A BODY
AT THE
IRISH
BOOK CLUB

BOOKS BY LUCY CONNELLY

A BODY
AT THE
IRISH
BOOK CLUB

Lucy Connelly

bookouture

Published by Bookouture in 2026

An imprint of Storyfire Ltd.
Carmelite House
50 Victoria Embankment
London EC4Y 0DZ

www.bookouture.com

The authorised representative in the EEA is Hachette Ireland
8 Castlecourt Centre
Dublin 15 D15 XTP3
Ireland
(email: info@hbgi.ie)

ISBN: 978-1-80550-151-0
eBook ISBN: 978-1-80550-150-3

This book is dedicated to GayLynn. Thank you for being my cheerleader.

ONE

As I arrived in the beautiful, stained-glass windowed train station in Shamrock Cove, the tightness that had strangled my chest for the last few weeks loosened its hold. I stepped off the train and took in the salt air and my shoulders dropped a good two inches.

Home.

"Miss McCarthy, I have your bags," the porter said from beside me.

"Oh, thanks. I can take it from here." I tried to tip him.

"I've got them," he said. "I was hoping you could sign my book for me."

I smiled. "Sure. But I'll sign it whether you carry my bags or not."

"It's my job, ma'am."

My sister Lizzie and I hadn't even lived here a year, but this was most definitely home. The people were friendly and kind. We'd grown to love the place. I'd been on a book tour for the last month, and I'd been able to travel the world, which had been fun and exhausting.

I was glad, though, to get back to my normal activities and

my own bed. Oh, and Mr. Poe, the best dog in the world, who happened to be waiting with my very excited sister in the train station.

Lizzie ran up and pulled me into a breath-stealing hug. "We missed you," she said. Mr. Poe yapped softly as if he agreed. When she loosened her hold, I bent down to pick him up.

"Was it fabulous and exciting? How amazing was it staying at the Ritz in Paris? Did you just love it?" Her cheeks were flushed, and it was more than obvious she was glad to have me home. I'd lived a solitary existence for years in Manhattan where no one cared if I made it home or not. That had all changed when we moved to Ireland.

Even though I enjoyed my solitude, I wouldn't give up living with my sister for anything. We had a perfectly lovely life with wonderful friends and a town full of quirky characters to inspire my writing—not to mention the stunning sea views.

"Yes. Very glamorous and yes, to answer your other questions."

We chuckled.

"Did I mention we are excited to have you back?" She glanced at the porter with my bags. I had taken two, because there had been several formal events along with the signings. I'd done more schmoozing in the last month than I had in years as an author. While I can be social, I'm very much an introvert. I was glad to be back in the one place where I could be myself.

"It's raining so I brought the car," she said.

I followed her out, still holding Mr. Poe. He licked my chin, which was a sign he really had missed me. I squeezed him gently. The little black ball of fur was one of my favorite beings.

The porter loaded my bags and held the umbrella while I signed his book and tipped him.

"Thank you," he said. "I can't wait for the next one."

We made the short drive down Main Street where Lizzie

parked near our bookstore. Caro was at the register as we passed through.

"The wandering author has returned. I can't wait to hear about your trip." She grinned as she waved.

"It's good to be home." And it was. I loved the smell of the books, and felt the tension of the last few weeks drop away when I walked into our store.

We walked to the back door. It was the fastest way to the court, which was hidden behind a giant stone wall where we lived in cottage Number Three. There were six homes in the private area, which used to be the bailey of the castle up on the hill. We had to pass through a secret door in the stone wall behind to get to our home.

The rain stopped as we arrived at the gate of our picket fence. "The garden looks amazing," I said. Flowers bloomed everywhere. My sister had the greenest of thumbs. I did not. "I had no idea there were so many flowers."

"I've been sharing cuttings with our little gang on the court. Wait until you see the backyard. Mr. Poe and I have been very busy. He's been scaring the rabbits and squirrels away from the new fairy gardens. He's very good at his job."

"I bet he is."

He yapped softly as if he understood every word.

We dragged my bags to my room on the first floor. I gazed longingly at my bed. I'd really missed it.

"I know you are tired, but don't forget we have the signing tonight with the book clubs."

I wasn't sure why I had to do the signing the day I arrived home, but I didn't want to upset my sister. She'd been through enough the past year. And after tonight, I was free to rest and write for the next two months. I actually looked forward to a normal routine.

"I haven't forgotten." My stomach growled loudly.

We laughed.

"Let me guess, you didn't wake up in time to have food on the train."

"It's like you know me."

She laughed again. "I have breakfast warming in the oven. Freshen up and I'll see you in a bit." She and Mr. Poe headed for the kitchen.

After putting my suitcases in the corner, I cleaned up a bit after my long night of travel. I had a sleeper car on the train, which I quite enjoyed. Except every time we stopped, I woke up.

I changed into my coffee mug pjs and headed to the kitchen. Food and a nap, and then I would be good to go.

Eight hours later I ran around my room trying to get ready. I'd hit the snooze on my phone one too many times, and I was about to be late for my book signing. Thankfully it was a two-minute walk away.

My phone dinged for the third time with my sister asking where I was.

Heading your way, I texted. I scooped up the messenger bag I kept my pens, stickers and bookmarks in, and ran out the door.

After passing through the stone wall, I walked the few steps to the back door of the bookshop. I used the keypad we'd added for security purposes to go inside. And then promptly bumped into my sister, who may have yelped.

"Sorry," I said. "I didn't mean to scare you."

She held an armload of my latest novel.

"It's okay, I'm just glad you are here. We have quite the crowd."

I frowned. "I thought it was just Lolly's book club." Lolly was our sweet neighbor and the queen of the town. She knew everyone and they respected her. She was also the grandmother of the local detective inspector, Kieran.

"Well, the other book clubs found out, and they all wanted to participate. Even the young adult group. But it's only a hundred or so people. Not everyone could come. That's why we moved it from Lolly's home to the bookstore."

I grinned. I'd planned on maybe signing ten or fifteen books for Lolly's club, but I was grateful. Readers had so many choices and I appreciated the love they showed me by buying my books. I was thankful for every single one of them.

"Okay," I said.

"You don't mind, do you? I thought it was sweet they were jealous and wanted to come."

"No. It's all good," I said.

Her shoulders dropped. "Good, that's a relief. I'll go settle everyone down. You can wait in the office and Caro will come get you for the introduction."

"You don't have to be so formal. These are our friends and neighbors."

"Right. Um. Well, it's also being filmed for the local newspaper's website. And we're putting it up on our online site so people can buy the autographed version if they like." She held up a hand. "And no, we aren't charging more. It's first come, first served for the online sales. I know how you feel about that."

I never liked it when authors charged more for autographed copies. If readers made the effort, so would I.

"You do know me better than anyone else."

She grinned. "I try. Now, I left you some coffee and cookies in my office. I had a feeling you'd be rushing and would forget dinner."

"Like I said, you know me best."

We laughed.

She headed off and I went into the office. It was immaculate. When we'd first arrived, there had been boxes surrounding the desk, and while it was clean, it didn't appear very organized. My sister had taken care of that over the last few months. She

was extremely organized in all things and was the most method-
ical person I knew.

I ate some of the chocolate chip cookies and drank the
coffee she left me. Normally, I would never drink caffeine after
two or so, but I needed my brain. Then I pulled up the reading I
was doing tonight. It was only a five-minute teaser. I never liked
to make people listen to something they could read just as
easily. But I'd do whatever the bookstore folks wanted,
including my sister. I understood how to write books; they knew
how to sell them.

I'd done this routine so many times over the last few
months, I was well familiar. Still, I was always nervous around
loads of people. My sister thrived in this kind of situation. I
preferred being alone in my office with my computer. Well, I
liked Mr. Poe's company when he was willing to leave my sister
behind.

Strange that we were twins and so very different.

Caro knocked on the open door. "Are you ready, big star?"

I snorted.

She grinned. "Your sister has been so excited about this."

"I've signed here before when we did the literary festival.
It's not a big deal."

"Ah, that's where you are wrong. It's a big deal to her." She
winked at me.

I followed Caro down the hallway. While she worked for
my sister, she'd become one of our best friends. She'd also been
the assistant to our grandfather and had lovely stories about
him. Even though we hadn't met him when he was alive, he'd
left a wonderful legacy for us. His friends, and our neighbors,
had so many stories they told us about him.

Less so about our father, but that was a story for another
day. I needed to concentrate on the night ahead.

We headed up the brass stairs. When we reached the top
step, Caro held up a hand for me to pause behind her. The

bookshop walls and shelves were painted a deep blue, and there were oddities spaced among the books. Some were antiques that my grandfather and sister picked up for décor. Others were sold along with the books. It had always reminded me of some grand library of a country gentleman, which fit since it had belonged to our grandfather.

My sister glanced over and smiled. "Ladies and gentlemen, I give you Mercy McCarthy."

There was applause, and I moved behind the podium. Lizzie and Caro had shifted some of the shelves to put more chairs in the open area upstairs at the bookshop. There were at least a hundred people there, possibly more as some stood in the back, our next-door neighbors, Rob, Scott, and Brenna among them.

I smiled and waved. "Hello, everyone. Thank you for coming out tonight. I'm grateful to you all. I'm so happy to be home. I hope you'll indulge me a bit, as I've been asked to do a reading." Then I launched into my spiel.

After the reading, I took questions. My sister had asked people to introduce themselves before asking.

"Hi, I'm Eva Walsh," said a gray-haired woman dressed in puce from the bow in her hair down to her slacks. I wondered if that was an Irish thing, as our friend Lolly often wore bright colors from head to toe as well. In fact, Lolly was in a purple top and matching linen slacks.

I smiled. "Hi, Mrs. Walsh. What's your question?"

"Is it true that you are the new girlfriend of our detective inspector?" the woman said.

I opened my mouth and closed it. Some in the room laughed, others gasped.

"Crazy woman," an older gentleman said.

"Stuff it, McCormick," Eva retorted.

"Eva, that's rude, even for you," Lolly said. She pointed a finger. "You shouldn't be asking things like that."

"Really, Eva. Even for you that's a bit much," another woman said. I'd seen her around town but couldn't remember her name. She was on a bunch of committees with my sister. She raised her eyebrows.

"Don't act like you aren't curious," Eva said. "You want to know more than I do. And at least they are single, unlike *some* people in this town." She harrumphed.

"I think it best if we keep these questions related to the author's book and writing," my sister said softly. She was kind, but we had always been staunch protectors of one another. "Do you have something related to the book?"

The woman smirked. "Fine. How many hours a day do you write?"

I took a deep breath. This was a much easier question to answer. While the detective inspector and I had been on a sort of date, it was cut short because of a crime. I had no idea how to define our relationship.

"It depends on how close I am to a deadline." The audience laughed. "But I try to get in a minimum of six hours a day and I try to take weekends off if the deadlines allow it." That was something new for me. But my sister had insisted on improving the quality of my life so that I wasn't a hermit like I'd been when I lived in Manhattan.

The woman who had chastised Eva spoke next. "My name is Marianne. I'd like to know how many more books you have planned for your detective, and if you use Shamrock Cove as inspiration?"

"I'm contracted for four more, and we'll see after that. And I'm taking the fifth on the inspiration question. I find it everywhere I look, to be honest."

Everyone who knew me smiled.

The remaining questions were mainly focused on my books, and it always amazed me how much readers remembered. I tend to write and then move on from the details of the last book.

A few times, I had to repeat the question while I gave myself time to remember the situations they asked about in previous books.

By the time I'd finished signing, it was nearly nine at night. It was all I could do not to yawn. My coffee had worn off an hour or so ago, and my hand had cramped. Though, I would never complain. I was well aware how awesome a privilege my job happened to be.

After a selfie with the last participant, Lizzie shuffled them toward the stairs.

"I know you are exhausted, but you did a wonderful job," she said to me. "I'm going to head downstairs and help Caro finish up the sales. Will you be okay?"

"Of course," I said. "I can help as well."

She shook her head. "We've got this. But if you could take Mr. Poe home for a romp, that would be great."

He lifted his head from beside my chair. He'd fallen asleep during the reading but had stayed near to me. I think he might have missed me while I was gone.

Lizzie went downstairs.

"You ready to head home?" I asked him.

He grunted. He followed me to the stairs but then stopped and sniffed the air. Then he turned back and cocked his head.

Mr. Poe growled. He seldom did that unless he sensed danger.

"What is it?" I whispered. "I know you don't like the stairs. I can carry you down."

The brass steps were slightly curved, and he wasn't a fan of going down them.

But when I reached down to pick him up, he backed away. Then he growled again and took off. I followed him. I couldn't imagine what might be wrong.

"Are you mad because I left you behind for so long? I brought you a toy. I just haven't unpacked everything."

He didn't listen.

We went around a corner to the young adult section. I found him standing a few feet from the woman who had asked me about Kieran—Eva Walsh. She sat with her head bent reading my book.

"Ma'am, Lizzie has asked that everyone move downstairs," I said softly.

She didn't move.

Mr. Poe sniffed and then yelped. He glanced back at me. I swear he was worried. The dog was more expressive than most humans.

My breath caught in my chest.

No. This is not happening.

"Eva, wasn't it? Can you hear me?"

Silence.

I moved slowly toward her and then knelt so I could look at her face. Her eyes were closed, and it appeared she was asleep. When I touched her neck to check for a pulse, she fell over. She was still warm, but she was long gone.

There was a small bruise on her neck, and I worried that I'd pressed too hard searching for some form of life.

There wasn't one.

"Oh. No. This isn't good."

Mr. Poe grunted as if he agreed.

TWO

After checking for a pulse again, I sniffed the air. Mainly, because Mr. Poe kept doing so. She was older, probably in her late seventies. Her rose perfume was strong, and I couldn't smell anything else.

I pulled my cell from my jacket pocket, and called Kieran, the detective inspector.

"Mercy? I thought you were already home. Didn't you have a signing tonight? What's wrong?" he asked worriedly. He and I had chatted a few times a week while I'd been gone. Mostly, we talked about cases he'd been working on, and how my trip was going. But I'd grown to look forward to our chats.

"Why do you think something is wrong? I could just be calling to chat."

"What happened? I can hear the strain in your voice."

I cleared my throat. Maybe he also knew me too well. "Mr. Poe found a dead body. It's Eva Walsh. Do you know her?"

There was a long pause.

"Where are you?"

"Second floor of the bookstore. My sister is still checking

people out downstairs. I don't want to mess things up for her, so can you be discreet."

"Mercy?"

"Yes?"

"A woman died. Things are going to be messy."

I sighed. "Right. She's older, though. It's probably natural causes." I leaned over Eva. "Except, I think there's something on her neck."

"I'll be there in five." He hung up.

I made a face, but I had to tell Lizzie before he arrived. I didn't want her to freak out in front of her customers.

I went to the stairs. "Lizzie, can you please come here. I need you," I said urgently.

She ran up the steps. "What's wrong?"

"I need you to take a deep breath," I said. "And then let it out."

She frowned. "I don't like this. You're managing me. What's going on?"

"Do what I asked, and I'll tell you."

She did. "What is it?" she whispered the words.

"Mr. Poe found Eva Walsh."

She stared at me like I had two heads. "Okaaay. Did you have an argument about the personal question she asked?"

"No. Uh. She wasn't able to talk."

Mr. Poe grumbled beside me.

She stared down at him, and then at me. Her eyes went wide. "She can't be dead. She was just asking questions."

I guided my sister to the chair she'd set up for me. Her face had gone white, and I worried about shock. It wasn't like I was used to finding dead bodies, but I wrote about crime and had to do some grisly research for my books. I was a bit more used to that sort of thing.

"I've already called Kieran. He's on his way."

"She's elderly, do you think it was natural causes?"

I cleared my throat again. "Well, maybe." I pursed my lips thinking about the bruise on her neck.

She shook her head. "No. No. She was not murdered in my bookstore. That can't happen—again. People will start thinking it's unlucky to shop here."

"Or they will like the idea that they might be murdered here. People are weird that way."

"Please don't make jokes."

"Sorry. You know my way of dealing with the morbid side of life is through dark humor."

She nodded. "Stop saying you're sorry. You didn't kill her."

"Did you?" Kieran asked behind me.

My sister and I jumped.

"Stop sneaking up on people, it's rude," I said.

He nodded toward me. "Show me where she is. Lizzie, I'll need to speak to you when we're done with the scene."

"Of course, is it okay to let the last few customers go? We're almost finished checking everyone out."

He frowned. "Yes. But I'll need your security feed and a list of everyone who was here tonight." He held up a hand. "It is probably natural causes, but we must do our due diligence."

He was always so professional. I'd grown to appreciate his mostly by the book way of doing things—and the way he sometimes let me in on what was happening.

She nodded. "That's simple enough. It was most of the folks from our book clubs. I'll put that together for you."

"If it's murder, shouldn't you keep people here?" I asked.

"I know Eva. She was dealing with COPD and had heart troubles, according to my gran. Do you really think the death is suspicious?" He glanced at me.

I shrugged. "I have no idea. You take a look and tell me."

I followed him around the corner. Sheila, his second in command, came up with a kit, and she was followed by a few others on Kieran's team of officers, as well as the EMTs. I stood back, watching, but trying to stay out of their way. I wondered if they would notice what I had.

One thing was for certain; the news would travel quickly since there were still customers in the store. That said, I prayed it was natural causes.

When one of the EMTs shook his head, Kieran moved forward, as Sheila snapped some photos.

Kieran examined Eva and then came back to me.

"Did you try CPR?"

I shook my head. "There was no sign of life, or I would have. I didn't want to. You know what happened last time I did CPR—it didn't go so well. I was waiting for the experts."

"That was smart of you, but you didn't do anything wrong the last time. By all accounts you tried to save the victim, but there was nothing you could do."

And it still continued to haunt me several months later.

"What makes you think this is a suspicious death?" he asked me.

"There is a mark on her neck. It looked like some sort of puncture. But I guess it could have also been a bee sting or something. Except, there was no swelling. And the bruise is light, like it just happened. Maybe I'm thinking like a mystery novelist, and making too much of it. She seemed fine during the signing. Like you said, she wasn't very healthy."

"Did you notice her talking with anyone? Was there an argument that made you think someone might hurt her?"

I shook my head. "I was busy signing books. I pretty much only see the reader in front of me. But there is..." I had to tell him. If I didn't mention it, his grandmother would.

"What is it?"

I sighed. "The first question she asked in front of everyone was if we were, uh, dating."

His eyes went wide. "What?"

"Yeah. Luckily, my sister, and your gran, jumped in and I

was able to avoid that one. But that was my first time meeting her. I mean, I've seen her with your grandmother a few times, but I didn't know her name until tonight. And she didn't seem mean, just super curious about... um, us."

His eyes widened. If there was a rock, I'd crawl under it.

He turned away. I didn't blame him. While I had to admit there was a connection between us, we were as far away from defining it as anyone could get.

"Right. I'll have the medical examiner do a full workup. We can't be too careful. I'm going to leave Sheila and the team to finish up here, but I need to inform the family."

That had to be one of the worst parts of his job.

"Do you know anything about the family? Did they get along with Eva?"

"They did. She was a busybody, but also beloved. Her family will be devastated."

I followed him downstairs. Everyone who had been at the signing was gone and only Caro, Lizzie, and Mr. Poe, were behind the counter.

"We weren't certain what we should do," Lizzie said.

"Give Sheila the keys, and she can lock up when the team is done," he said. "But first I have a few questions. Did you notice anything strange tonight, in regard to Eva?"

"Other than she asks rather personal questions, no," Caro said in her straightforward way.

"I told him about that," I said.

My sister chewed on her lip, but I knew she tried to hide a grin. She was well aware how embarrassing this had to be for Kieran and me.

"Did she speak with anyone else? Have any sort of argument?"

Lizzie's eyebrows scrunched together. "Why, do you think her death was suspicious?"

"These are normal questions when someone dies," he said calmly. "I'm covering the bases, as you Yanks like to say."

"She and Lolly had words," Caro said. "They were in the corner, and I don't think Lolly liked the question Eva had asked. There was some finger wagging and eyebrow lifting. After that, I don't remember seeing Eva again."

He nodded. "Anyone else?"

"I was busy helping my sister with the crowd," Lizzie said. "And I thought everyone had gone downstairs. I have no idea why she was back in the YA section."

"YA?" He seemed confused.

"Young adult," we all said at the same time.

"You said she was sick. She may not have been feeling well, and that's a comfortable bench," I said. I didn't want Lizzie worrying unnecessarily.

She nodded. "That poor family. Clara, her granddaughter, is in here all the time with Eva. They share a love of books."

"Was she here tonight?" he asked.

"For a bit," Caro said. "After Mercy spoke, she had to get home. She has four young ones, two of them still at home. Eva stood in line to have all of their books signed."

While most of the signing was a blur, I did remember Eva, and signing the name Clara to one of the copies she'd held in her arms.

"If you think of anything else out of the ordinary, please let me or Sheila know. I need to head over to tell the next of kin."

"Oh, that's a terrible part of your job." Lizzie shook her head. "Would you like us to go with you? I could help look after Clara's children. They are teens, but still. I have some extra biscuits and baked goods from the signing. We can take those over. If that's all right with you, Kieran?"

"I. Uh. Sure." He seemed confused.

All I wanted to do was go home and sleep, but my sister had

a tender heart. I followed her back to the office to help gather the baked goods.

"I'm getting better at this," she whispered.

"What do you mean?" I asked, completely confused.

"Finding ways to get close to the family so you can investigate."

I gasped. "Lizzie."

She shrugged. "Hey. Someone died in my store. Except for that question she asked tonight—and she was right, we all want to know—she was a lovely customer and if anything bad happened, we need to know."

Well, this was new. Usually, she wanted me as far away from investigations as possible. Though, she'd grown very protective of the store and of the people in town.

And if someone had murdered poor Eva, the faster we found the killer, the better.

THREE

After dropping Mr. Poe at home, we rode in Kieran's police SUV the few miles out of town to Clara's farm. I had to force my eyes open on the short drive, as I'd grown increasingly tired as he headed down the dark roads. I tried to stifle a yawn, and Kieran grinned.

"You didn't have to come along," he said.

"Of course we do," Lizzie said from the back seat. She'd insisted I sit in front with the detective inspector. "These are friends, and they've lost someone special."

"I only meant that Mercy appears a bit tired from her travels."

"Oh, I didn't think about that. Are you okay?" She leaned forward and touched my shoulder.

"I'm fine. Do we know anything about the family? Other than they like to shop at the bookstore?"

"I've known Mrs. Walsh since I was a wee one," he said. "The family owns one of the markets in town and their farms are organic. They also have a yarn business. Gran could tell you more about that. She and Mrs. Walsh were always knitting."

"I didn't know they owned the organic grocery store," Lizzie said. "I've only seen teens running the register."

"Right. Those are Clara's youngest kids," he said. "There are four of them. Two are at university, and the younger ones help run the store and farm. As far as teens go, they are responsible kids. Jeremy is their da. He's a good sort, though he likes his drink. He was in a fair bit of trouble in his younger years but seems to have matured. Nice family of hard workers. At least, as far as I know."

"So, if it was murder, no suspects in the family?"

He shook his head. "I can't imagine it. They are kind folk, and they loved her. At least, according to my gran. I called her from the store. She and her group will be bringing more food and support tomorrow for the family."

"I love this town," my sister said wistfully. "The way people look out for one another. It's not like anywhere I've ever known. I mean, I thought people in Texas were kind, but the Irish go beyond for their friends."

I couldn't shake the feeling that Eva had been killed. Call it gut intuition, which Kieran wasn't crazy about, but I just knew her death had something to do with the bruise on her neck. "How about some sort of money angle, maybe an inheritance. I mean, with all those businesses there may have been some trouble."

He shrugged. "I can't imagine she had anything worth killing over. And you'll see the family isn't like that. Like I said, I can't see them hurting her. They are going to be devastated."

It wasn't long before he turned off on a dirt road. The rain had turned it to mud and we fishtailed a couple of times, but Kieran had it under control.

"When do you think the autopsy will be done?" I asked.

"In the next twenty-four to forty-eight hours, depending on tests," he said. "We're first up after they finish the one they are working on now."

"That's faster than usual."

"It is. After complaints from families in some of the smaller towns, they've added to the staff at the medical examiners."

"I seem to remember signing a petition," Lizzie said. "Your gran set it up."

He laughed. "She has more influence than she would ever admit. And the powers-that-be are a bit afraid of her, I believe."

"Good for Lolly," I said. I wasn't surprised. His grandmother was the kindest of souls, but she was also a force of good for the town of Shamrock Cove and its residents.

When he pulled up, it was in front of an adorable thatched-roof cottage in a Tudor style, not unlike our own. The place was surrounded by flowers and little fairy houses glowed near some of the trees.

"It's like an enchanted garden," Lizzie said. "I want to do this in our backyard."

"It is beautiful and if anyone can do it, you can," I said. "You have made a decent start already."

"I was bored while you were gone. I just kept adding to it."

"Well, it's beautiful." I glanced back and she smiled.

The rain had paused, though there were still dark clouds overhead. Making the night even darker.

Then it hit me. We were about to tell someone they'd lost a loved one. I took a deep breath.

Kieran knocked on the bright-pink door. There were large picture windows on each side of the door, making the front door look like a smiling face.

"Just a minute," someone called from inside. "Don't cheat. Put it on pause," the voice said.

When the door opened, a red-headed woman with curls piled on top of her head smiled. "Kieran? What are you doing out this late? Jeremy and I are trying to beat our youngest at *Knights of Honor*. He's whipped the pants off us, though. Do you want to join us? Caleb would love that."

Kieran took a breath. "Can we go inside, I have some news for you," he said. It was then she seemed to notice my sister and me standing behind him.

She frowned and took a step back. "No. It's Gran, isn't it? I wondered why she wasn't answering my calls. I thought maybe she'd called it a night and stayed with Lolly. Is she in jail again?" She peeked around Kieran. "I'm sorry she asked you such a personal question. I had a text from a friend of mine. I was glad I left. I would have been so embarrassed. Did you press charges?" She glanced back at Kieran. "I don't understand. Can she do that? I'll admit Gran could be rude, but that's no reason to put her in jail."

He cleared his throat. "Clara, she's not in jail. Can we come inside? I think it best if we sit down."

Her hand flew to her mouth, but she nodded. Then she opened the door wider.

We followed her into their living area. They called them snugs here. There was a large television on the wall, with a video game paused. A man and his younger look-alike son, turned to see who was at the door. The older gentleman's eyes grew larger, as if he knew.

"Turn the game off, Caleb."

"But we aren't..." the boy said.

A look from his father, and he turned off the console and the television.

The man jumped up and waved a hand. "Have a seat and tell us what's happened."

He glanced behind Kieran at us, as if he couldn't quite understand why we were there. I didn't blame him.

"It's your gran," Kieran said to Clara. "She's passed on, but there isn't much I can tell you. We don't have all the details yet. I'm so very sorry for your loss."

Clara put her face in her hands and sobbed. Her husband moved to hug her. And her son hit the floor in front of her. His head on her lap. He was a teen, but there were tears in his eyes.

"Was it her COPD?" the father asked. "Clara got on to her earlier this evening because she refused to take her oxygen tank when she was out in public. Said she didn't like people thinking she was old." He shook his head. "But she's been having terrible asthma on top of everything else she had going on."

Kieran shook his head. "I really can't say. Because it was sudden, we'll be doing a brief investigation into the cause. I know that will help settle your mind. Lolly wanted me to say how very sorry she is. She'll be out tomorrow along with her crew for anything you might need."

"Can you tell us where, at least?" Clara asked.

"It will be common knowledge by the time we leave here, so I don't see the harm," he said. "It was at the bookstore. But I can assure you, Lizzie and her sister had nothing to do with it. That said, they wanted to come and offer their condolences."

"We know it's late," Lizzie said as she put a basket full of goodies on their coffee table. "But we wanted to tell you how very sorry we were. We adored Mrs. Walsh. She's always been so supportive of our store. Please, let us know if there is anything we can do for you. Would you like a cuppa? I can make one for you."

Clara nodded.

"Caleb, why don't you go help," the father said.

The boy nodded and jumped to his feet. Lizzie picked up the basket and followed him to the kitchen.

"I want to preface these questions with we do this with any sudden death," Kieran said. "It's standard. I'm not assuming there was any foul play, but I need all the facts so we can tie this up as quickly as possible. If it's okay, I need to ask you a few questions."

I'd been standing by the fireplace but moved to hand Clara a packet of tissues I kept in my messenger bag. I never knew what I might need at a book signing, so it had become a bit of a Mary Poppins bag. Especially when I was traveling.

"Thank you," she said hoarsely. "I can't believe this. She was just joking that we shouldn't wait up late for her in case she found her a man. That was code for she was staying at Lolly's. She did that sometimes, so we didn't have to go pick her up when she was running late in town. I texted to see if she was okay, but she didn't answer. I just assumed she was having fun." She sobbed. "She seemed fine at the bookstore. The doctors said it could be any time, but I didn't think it would be this fast. She was determined to live her life on her terms. Oh, Gran."

That was strange. I hadn't seen a phone on her person. Though, it might have been in the small purse she'd carried. The books she had signed had been in a tote she'd brought with her. I'd have to ask Kieran if I could go through the bag later.

"I'd like to ask about her health first," he said.

Clara took a deep breath. "As you know, we moved in with her two years ago. The house had become too much for her, and we needed more space. She had COPD and was finding it difficult to keep up with things. Jeremy built a room on the back of the kitchen for her. We didn't want her going up and down the stairs. She had arthritis, as well. And an irregular heartbeat, the doctors thought she might need a pacemaker soon, but she said she was too old for surgery. She didn't want anyone cutting into her. Maybe her heart just gave out. I can't believe she's gone." She sobbed again and stuck her face back in her hands.

"I'll be quick," Kieran said. "Jeremy, as far as you know, she didn't have any problems with others?"

Jeremy frowned. "Do you mean did she have an enemy who would do her harm?"

Kieran nodded.

He glanced at the fireplace as if he wanted to say something but thought twice about it.

"Anything you can share will help."

"Well, she didn't have any filters, as you know," Jeremy said. "Some people do not always like hearing the unvarnished truth. But I can't see someone wanting to harm her for it. She was an old woman who spoke her mind, there's more than one of those around here."

"True," Kieran said. "Had she mentioned having words with anyone?"

"She was always prattling on about some sort of gossip," he said. "I tuned her out most of the time."

"Jeremy. That's not fair," Clara admonished.

"Sorry, luv, but it's true," Jeremy said. "Again, I can't imagine anyone wanting to hurt her over it. Like Clara said, her health wasn't the best. I'm sure it was natural causes. Unless there is something that makes you think it wasn't?"

I glanced at him. There was something in his eyes I couldn't quite pinpoint.

I wondered if Kieran had caught that look. Maybe the man grieved for his grandmother-in-law. But I wasn't certain.

"As I said, we always investigate a sudden death. Only doing my due diligence."

"Here we are." Lizzie came in with a huge tray of tea. "Caleb helped me make a pot of chamomile. We thought something calming might be good this late in the evening."

"She brought all kinds of baked goods, Ma. Including your favorite chocolate chip scones," Caleb said.

Clara sniffed. "That's very kind of you."

"No problem at all. As we said, we adored your grandmother. She kept the book club discussions lively."

"Thank you, again," Clara said.

"I'm grateful to you all," Jeremy said. "But I'd like some time to grieve with my family. If that's okay, Kieran?"

The detective inspector stood. "Of course, and again, so sorry for your loss."

She nodded.

"Oh, where's Quinn?"

Clara's hand went to her mouth. "Oh. She's staying with a friend. Jeremy?"

"I'll collect her, luv. Don't worry."

Jeremy walked us to the door.

"If you think of anything, please let me know," Kieran said.

The other man nodded and shut the door quickly behind us.

After we were in the car, he'd driven half a mile when he paused on the side of the road.

"You saw something," he said.

"It was the husband and only for a few seconds," I said. "He's hard to read, but it appeared as though he thought of something. And he didn't want to tell us about it."

"Caleb told me that his great-gran was upset over something that happened at bingo last week," Lizzie added. "According to the story, his gran and some man nearly came to blows when she thought he cheated."

"Would someone kill another person over bingo?" I asked.

"Unfortunately, it could happen," Kieran said. "As you well know, people have been killed for less. And reputations can be important around here."

I blew out a breath. "Wow. I hope it wasn't that."

"By chance did he mention a name?" Kieran asked.

"Actually, Caleb said Eva thought it was some sort of conspiracy with Harold McCormick and Marianne Gilbreth," Lizzie continued. "His gran thought they were out to get her. Her great-grandson made her sound paranoid. I know them all. I can't see it, though."

"Were they both there tonight?"

"Yes," she said. "But I don't remember them even talking to Mrs. Walsh. She was too busy asking pointed questions of our famous writer."

I cleared my throat. "She was one of the first in line to get her books signed." I changed the subject. I didn't want to spend any time discussing that particular question, again. "But I have no idea what she was doing after that."

"Did she say anything else to you?" he asked.

"No. Just who she wanted the books autographed to. She was giving a couple of them as gifts. I had a lot of books to sign, so we were rushing through the line."

"I have to admit, I don't remember seeing her either. I was busy helping with those coming up in the line. I can say they are all fairly chatty when it comes to the book club and that Mr. McCormick makes a point of disagreeing with everyone else, no matter their stance on the subject. But he behaved tonight. Perhaps because he's quite a fan of my sister."

I snorted.

"It's true," she said. "You signed every single book he brought; the whole collection."

"Oh, that's him. He seemed perfectly nice to me. He even wanted a selfie."

"He's a curmudgeon," Kieran said. "Had him for chemistry class years ago. He was always an angry man. He'd been a chemist, well, I think you call them pharmacists. I never understood why he was so mean. But he forced us to learn, so he had that going for him. When he retired the second time, he took over the local garden center in town."

"He had a cane, right? I seem to remember him waving it at someone."

"That's him," Lizzie said. "Though, he's always flirted a bit with Caro and me. I've bought a lot of plants from him. He's a funny man, but I could see him holding a grudge. And I can see what Kieran says about him being a curmudgeon, but definitely not a killer. He's very knowledgeable when it comes to the right mix of soil and plants. Everything he's suggested has worked."

"But if he was a chemist back in the day, he might know how to kill someone," I said.

"There is that," Lizzie said softly.

Kieran might not believe me, but I was certain. Someone had killed poor Eva, and I was going to figure out who it was.

FOUR

The next morning, I texted Kieran, who said he was busy with another case. I'd planned on writing most of the day, but I couldn't get poor Eva Walsh out of my head. Had she been murdered? Kieran didn't know yet, but he expected the autopsy soon. Though, that could be today or a few days from now. Time wasn't experienced the same way here as it was in Manhattan.

I was too antsy to write. Part of it was I'd been going like the Road Runner for more than a month, and things were too quiet. Lizzie had taken Mr. Poe to work with her. I needed a walk. I swore to myself that it wasn't because Mr. McCormick had a garden center up the road. I thought maybe I could pick up a few plants for the fairy garden and surprise Lizzie.

Okay, and I could nose around a bit. What I couldn't do was sit and write. I changed into jeans and a sweater. After looking out the window, I realized I'd be better off wearing my wellies. I slipped on the new forest-green ones I'd bought before I'd gone on the tour.

Even though it was raining, Rob was outside in his garden.

"I'm headed to the garden center to pick up some stuff for Lizzie. Do you want to come with me?"

He grinned. "Are you going to grill Mr. McCormick?"

I made a noise. "Of course... not. I'm going to buy some gifts. Lizzie's been working hard."

"Rigggght. It has nothing to do with the fact that he and Eva Walsh turned bickering in to a new art. Their one-liners are legendary. Let me get my mac and wellies, we're getting more rain today."

"Isn't that every day in Ireland?"

He chuckled as he sat on the bench just inside his front door and put on his wellies. "This time of year, yes. I heard you went to tell poor Clara about her gran last night."

News traveled fast in this town. "She was so upset. My heart hurt for her."

"I only met Mrs. Walsh a few times. She thought my food was too spicy. But Clara and her kids visit the food truck just about every time I'm open. She's a sweetheart. I've got a couple of her favorite pizzas and a roast I'm taking over later on."

"We are so lucky to have a world-famous chef in town."

He snorted. I made the same sound when I received compliments.

"You're the famous one. You were on the news a few times a week. Scott and I were cheering you on. People were lined up around the block in London, Amsterdam, and Milan. That had to feel good."

"Were they? I had no idea. I just sign books for everyone and then it's off to the next stop. I never see the news. I'm always cratered after a signing. It's a room service dinner and then crashing. Though, I do sometimes ask the driver to take me past some of the more famous spots on the way back. Oh, I met up with my editor in London. She was there for a book fair. But enough about me. Lizzie texted that your publisher loved your new cookbook."

Rob was half Korean, but he cooked food from all over the world. I'd never had a dish I didn't like from him.

"It was a huge relief. You never know when you send it to your editor how they will feel about your book."

"So very true. I feel nauseous every time I send something," I said.

"Do you? After all the books you've written, that surprises me."

"Imposter syndrome never goes away, at least from what I've heard. I know that is true for me."

When he pushed through the secret door in the wall, we jumped. Brenna stood there. She stepped back. "You scared me." She held her grocery bags up in a defensive posture.

"I guess we are all a little jumpy," Rob said.

"Where are you two headed?" She smiled. Today she was dressed in a long sweater and jeans. She worked as a photographer, but she was beautiful enough to be a model. That said, she was as beautiful on the inside as she was on the outside.

"Mercy is off to find out if Mr. McCormick is a murderer."

"What?" Her eyes were wide. "Was Mrs. Walsh murdered?"

"We don't know," I said. I held up a hand. "I'm gathering information just in case."

"But you think it's a murder. That's why you're talking to people who were there last night, right? You think someone killed that poor woman," Rob said.

"I—you were both there. Did you notice anything funny?" It wasn't worth arguing because they were right, and we all knew it.

"It was crowded," Brenna said. "We were helping to hand out numbers so the elderly could sit until their numbers were called. That was your sister's idea. She's always looking out for people in this town. You both are, just in different ways. You find murderers and she emanates kindness."

Maybe I could have taken offense, but she was right. People were drawn to my sister because of that. But we were also from Texas, and she never let others take advantage of her. She was much stronger than she'd ever give herself credit for, and I admired that strength.

"She does. And I'm going to buy her some plants. Nothing more."

"Uh. Huh. Right. Let me drop off my shopping. I get left out of the Scooby Gang antics too often because I'm always working out of town. I want to come along."

I couldn't help but laugh. They'd been calling themselves that for some time. And, to be honest, they had helped many times with investigations. It was great to have spies around town.

After she dropped her things, we headed around the corner to Main Street. It was only a block and a half up. There was a store front on Main Street and behind it was an enormous greenhouse. It was called Bláthanna, which was Gaelic for flowers, and I'd been here a few times with my sister. She loved this place. That said, I'd never seen Mr. McCormick here. I'd had no idea he was the owner.

He stood behind the front counter, repotting what looked like a small rose bush. *"Dia duit,"* he said in Irish Gaelic. Lizzie and I tried to learn some of the language, but it was incredibly difficult.

He wore an explorer's hat and khakis like a character from an Indiana Jones movie. "Good morning," I said. "Thank you for coming to the signing last night."

"Why wouldn't I? We have a famous author right here in Shamrock Cove and your sister made it clear we should support all authors. Though, I have to admit, I was a fan before you two landed in our fair town. Unlike those other hangers-on."

I grinned. "Thank you."

He glanced behind me at Rob and Brenna. "Is there a garden club meeting someone forgot to tell me about?"

I smiled. "I'm actually here for a gift for Lizzie. Since I'm not a gardener, I thought my friends could help me out."

He grinned. "And here I thought you'd come to question me about Eva, God rest her soul." He made the sign of the cross.

"Should I be questioning you?" I said it like a joke, and from his expression he took it as such.

"We did like to argue, I'll give you that. But I can't imagine anyone wanting to harm the poor woman. Did they, though? Was she murdered?"

"Why do you ask that?"

"You're here under the guise of buying your sister a gift, and I heard you were asking some rather pointed questions of the family last night."

This town and its gossip.

"I was only there to support Kieran, as his officers were otherwise engaged." I didn't want him to be on guard. I'd hoped to be a bit sneaky.

"Well, you can tell him that if it was murder, I had nothing to do with it."

"Can you tell me about the arguments?"

"I might. What are you here to buy?" His eyebrows rose.

I grinned. "Like I said, some plants or flowers for Lizzie. She loves the fairy gardens around here and wants to turn our backyard into one."

"Follow me," he said. "Grace, watch the front. I'm headed out back," he said loudly.

"Got it, boss," a female voice said from an office off to the side.

We went out the back door, crossed the alley and went into the huge greenhouse in the back. The scent of dirt and plants filled my senses. The place was calming in a way. I liked sitting in our garden, but I wasn't allowed to touch the plants.

His stride was quick, as we followed him down one of the long aisles.

"Ask me what you will," he said.

"I was curious what you two argued about. I heard you didn't get along. And that maybe there was a problem at bingo the other night."

He grunted. "I didn't mind the woman, but she was always in everyone's business. She tried to tell me more than once how to advise gardeners. No one knows plants like me. And I don't boast, though that is the Irishman's prerogative. I've been working with plants since before I could walk. Me ma had my hands in the dirt right along with her when I was a wee one. It's in my blood. I know how to heal people with them, as well."

I decided to play dumb. "Did you have an apothecary?"

He shook his head. "I was a chemist, and I still own the apothecary in town. Though, I'm hands off at this point. When I retired from the store, I taught for a few years. But the young have no respect these days. My cousin was selling the garden center, so I bought it. Haven't looked back. I learned long ago that a man who sits idle dies from it. I keep busy with my business and other endeavors."

I wondered what those other endeavors included. If a drug had been used to kill Eva, he would have had access as well.

"And Eva gave you trouble."

"Eva was always going on about something. Now, here's a good start for your sister. It's *Sagina subulata* or Irish moss. She will have to tame it a bit, but she's a fair gardener." He handed me a pot of the green plant with tiny white flowers.

"Thanks," I said. "Any others?"

"Oh, we're just getting started. Young Rob, can you grab a cart?"

Rob nodded and made his way to the corner where several carts were in a row.

"What was your last argument about?"

He paused and then shook his head. He huffed, but turned and grinned. "Well, I called her on her rude behavior with you at the bookstore. That was not right, her asking about your love life in front of a crowd. But that was the way she was. She liked the shock value and to make people talk. She had no shame that way. We had a huge row at garden club last week. And another one at bingo. Was that last week or the one before? It all runs together."

"Oh? And?"

"Isn't what you're thinkin'," he said. "We mostly argued about the plants. She believed that gardens should always be formal. Like your sister, I'm a fan of a wild and natural look. We were arguing over an episode of the *Chelsea Flower Show* from last spring. She was like a terrier, never let things go. Even when she was obviously wrong."

We followed him down another aisle. "Ah, here you go." He handed me some colorful flowers in three different pots. I handed them to Rob and Brenna, who smiled. Then they sat them on the cart.

"I recognize the violets, what is the other one?"

"Dwarf cornflowers," he said. "Good pollinators. And you'll be needing some herbs. Fairies love a herb." We went to the far back corner. I would never admit it to my sister, but I sort of loved how people around here talked about fairies like they were among us.

"Do you know of anyone who might have wanted to cause Mrs. Walsh harm?"

He stopped and I nearly ran into him. Brenna ran into me, and Rob stopped us both from falling over.

Thanks, I mouthed.

Rob nodded.

"Like I said before, I can't imagine anyone wanting to hurt her. She'd give the shirt off her back, if need be. In her way, she was kind. She always thought she was right—about everything.

It was her nature. She liked to keep things uneven, if you understand my meaning. She kept people on their toes with her pointed comments. But, no, I can't imagine anyone wanting to hurt her. Was she murdered? Is that what this is about? I can't believe someone would take it that far."

"Uh. I have no idea, really," I said. "Kieran is investigating though."

"Well, I hope that isn't true. Last thing this town needs is another murder. If I think of something, I'll let the detective inspector know." He snapped his fingers. "Here, let's add some rosemary, thyme and oregano. They are pretty and tasty."

He stopped again and then turned to me.

"What is it?"

"That night at the bookstore, she looked a bit pale and was sweating. She also slurred her words when I spoke to her. I thought she and Lolly had hit the wine again."

"Oh? I didn't notice any of that."

He shrugged. "I just remember thinking it odd that she seemed tipsy. I asked if she was drunk because of the slurring. She told me to stuff it and stalked off. That's the last time I saw her."

Did she have a bag? I'd forgotten to ask Kieran the night before. I remembered the book in her hands, but I'd been so shocked to find her dead that I hadn't taken in the scene close to her. I needed to ask Kieran about the evidence they found around her.

Mr. McCormick was still on my list. He hadn't said anything that made me want to take him off. But he didn't seem angry enough to commit murder. More that he enjoyed his lively discourse with the deceased. His voice caught a few times. I had a feeling he would miss Eva, even though she drove him mad.

By the time we were done, I'd spent a fair amount of money, and we had to borrow one of Mr. McCormick's trolley to cart everything home. Rob promised him he'd bring it back, as he and Brenna had also bought some plants.

Back out on the street, they paused.

"What is it?"

"We want to know why you think she was murdered," Brenna asked.

"I never said that."

They grinned.

"Right," Rob said. "But you wouldn't be so curious about her if the death wasn't suspicious."

"You can't tell anyone, promise me." I trusted them, but I had to say it out loud. "I know you'll tell Scott, but I'd like to keep this between us. Maybe, don't mention it to Lolly until we are certain how she died. She was dear friends with poor Eva."

"We promise," Brenna said.

Rob pushed the trolley down the sidewalk, and we crossed the street.

"I have no idea what it means, but I noticed a bruise on her neck. And I took a picture with my phone. I could swear there was some sort of small puncture mark, but that is it. That's the only reason why I think there might have been foul play. Though it's interesting she was sweating and slurring her words. Maybe there was some sort of drug in her system. There was only tea and coffee being served at the store. Though, I suppose she could have had some alcohol before she arrived."

"Okay, what else? I mean, no offense," Rob said, "but she had a lot of health problems. Word is she was a walking time bomb, and I know that's a horrible thing to say."

"No, you're right. Clara told us the same thing about her grandmother's health. But she seemed to argue with everyone. It's easy to make enemies with a personality like that." I tried to avoid conflict, though I was never afraid of standing up for myself, my family, or friends.

"We can vouch for the garden club arguments," said Rob.

"We're doing a program at the Autumn Festival to bring in new members. How to Grow Your Garden in the Autumn and Winter. As he said, she was very regimented in her ideas about what that means. But she wasn't just arguing with him. Most of the members feel the same way as Mr. McCormick."

"I hate saying this about a dead woman, but I think most of us tolerated her because of her age," Brenna said. "I've heard people say she was kind, like Mr. McCormick, but I don't remember a time I've been around her when she wasn't making someone else uncomfortable. When will you know for sure if there was foul play?"

"As soon as the medical examiner's report comes in," I said. "Kieran doesn't think it will take as long as it does normally. I hope I'm wrong."

"Me too." Brenna crossed her arms. "I don't like the idea of a killer running around."

"Agreed," Rob said.

"Another name was mentioned. I think it was Marianne Gilbreth. Do you know her?"

"She's the current president of the garden club, and she was there last night," Rob said. "She and Mrs. Walsh did argue quite a bit. She works part-time at the church up the way as the secretary there. Not that she needs to. Her husband left her well-off. But she always says she likes to keep busy."

"Hmmm."

"You're trying to think of a way to speak to her, aren't you?" Brenna asked.

"You all are far too good at reading my mind."

"Well, you could join one of the many clubs she's in," Rob said.

"You know how bad I am at gardening. My sister barely lets me water the plants. I have two black thumbs."

"But she's also on the town committee for the Autumn

Festival. We're all on it, as well," Brenna grinned. "You should join us at the meeting tonight."

"Don't you have to be appointed to something like that?"

She shook her head. "We're always looking for more volunteers. But be warned, she will put you in charge of something. She will also ask you about how it's going every time she sees you. Marianne never forgets anything. You think your sister is super organized, but Marianne takes it to a whole new level."

I remembered a woman saying something to Eva. "Tall woman, with dark hair? She has a white streak in the front."

"Yes, that's her," Rob said.

I had a lot of writing to do, but some due diligence wouldn't hurt. And I liked the idea of contributing to the town. My sister was on several committees, but I always begged off, citing work. I would be home for the next few months, and the fall fête was a couple of weeks away.

If someone had really killed that poor woman, I was determined to find out who.

FIVE

By the time my sister made it home that night, I'd showered and dressed for the meeting about the fall fête. We were grabbing dinner at the pub after, so I'd eaten an apple to tide me over and was throwing it in the trash when she came into the kitchen.

She frowned. "Are you going somewhere?"

"Yes, I meant to text you earlier. I want to join the Autumn Festival committee."

She frowned, and then her eyes went wide. "You think someone on the committee killed poor Mrs. Walsh."

I shrugged. "I just want a chance to talk to people. And before you become too judgy, come outside. I have something to show you."

She sighed. "What now?"

I opened the back door, and Mr. Poe ran out into the yard chasing off some bird intruders.

Hesitantly, Lizzie peeked out and I waved a hand toward the plants I'd stacked on the deck.

Her hand went to her chest, and she gasped. "What is all of this?" She ran over to touch the leaves and flowers.

"You said you wanted a bigger fairy garden. The one by the

bench is somewhat small. I visited the garden center to pick up some plants for you. I may have also ordered some fairy houses online. They will be here in a few days and are solar-powered."

She hugged me hard. "This is wonderful, thank you. I can't wait to plant them. I'll call Caro and see if she can cover for me in the morning. They should go into the ground as quickly as possible."

"I could help out at the store in the morning. I'd probably be more useful there than here."

She cocked her head and grinned. "You might be right about that."

"Stab, straight to the heart."

She giggled. "Thank you again for the wonderful gift."

"I really missed you when I was gone," I said. "I'm used to us spending more time together, now. It felt weird without my other half."

"Oh, Mercy. That might be the sweetest thing you've ever said to me. And I missed you, too."

Mr. Poe barked, and we chuckled.

"He did, as well," she said. "Give me five minutes to freshen up, and I'll be ready to head to the committee meeting. I pray you don't have suspects there. I've been working with these people for months."

I shrugged. "I don't even know if Eva was murdered yet. I haven't heard back from Kieran. So, no need to worry. Think of this as my way of helping out the town, which has given us so much."

She laughed.

"What's so funny?"

"You almost sound sincere."

"Mean."

She giggled again.

. . .

Ten minutes later we were ready to head to Lolly's house on the court. I hadn't realized the meeting would be so close.

"Are you certain I'm not intruding?" I said.

"Not at all," she said. "We bring new volunteers to every meeting. You know how much work it takes for these things. The summer one nearly killed us because we didn't have enough help and several of us were doing triple duty."

I didn't know, because I'd been neck deep into the investigation of a killer. I did, however, have my first date back then with Kieran, which was cut short because of said investigation.

"What's your take on Marianne Gilbreth?"

"I like her," she said. "She isn't mean, but she keeps people on track. You know how folks like to hear themselves talk around here. As soon as someone starts speaking, she turns on a timer and gives them a minute. It sounds harsh but it's necessary. They will drone on for an hour if given a chance. At least, some of them. She's extremely organized and the woman loves a pie chart. But like I said, I appreciate that sort of thing."

My sister had many of those same traits.

After locking up the house, and putting Mr. Poe on his lead, we walked over. We knocked and were greeted by a bark from the lovely Bernard, Lolly's Irish wolfhound. The huge monster was her protector and stood guard whenever she had one of her narcoleptic episodes.

Mr. Poe danced beside me. He and Bernard had become great friends. Since Lolly loved animals, all pets were welcome at her house.

"Come in," someone called. We opened the door. Bernard sat regally to the right as if to greet us. I swear he and Mr. Poe nodded to one another.

Lolly was dressed head to toe in pink. She wore a pink sweater set, with the same color jeans and shoes. I loved that she was vivacious in her dress and personality.

"It's going to rain, so we're a bit stuffed in my snug, but grab some food and a chair. Glad you could join us, Mercy. We need everyone we can get for the fête." If she was suspicious of my reasons for being there, she didn't act like it.

"Happy to help," I said. I followed Lizzie into the dining area where a buffet had been set up on Lolly's beautifully decorated table. The Irish lace tablecloth was so pretty, I would have been worried about people spilling on it. There was a crystal candelabra and real china plates and silver. No paper plates or plastic forks for Lolly.

This was Shamrock Cove, so it was an incredible display of food and drinks. Everyone had brought a bit of something; they were always trying to outdo one another. The Irish knew how to throw a party, even a casual one that was supposed to be a meeting.

"I don't think we'll need that pub dinner after all," I said.

Lizzie grinned. "I always forget it's like a smorgasbord at these things. I feel bad for only bringing cookies."

"But they are the best cookies in the world."

She chuckled. "We might be a bit prejudiced when it comes to Mom's recipe."

"Maybe, but they are still the tastiest."

Rob and Brenna were on the other side of the table.

"Where is Scott?" I asked Rob.

"He had to fly to London for a new client. I'm on my own off and on for the next two weeks. I won't know what to do with myself. I already miss him, and he just left."

"Why didn't you go with him?" I asked.

He made a face. "When he's working I don't want him worrying about if I'm having a good time. If I'm there, I want to go to the theater at night, and he's always too exhausted. Besides, I have so many commitments here. It wouldn't be right since the council and the town have been so supportive of my new business. I want to give back."

He'd been trying to get his food truck going for years, and his permissions had finally gone through a few months ago.

"I would have gone to the theater by myself," Brenna said. "But then I'm selfish and I don't have a wonderful partner like you. So, maybe you're on to something."

"And if you get lonely, you can always hang out with us," Lizzie said. "We love company."

"Gather your food and let's take our seats," a woman said, and then she clapped her hands. "I want to start on time."

People were quick to follow her orders.

"That's Marianne, right?" I asked. She had dark hair and was wearing a green, belted button-down with a floral scarf tied artfully at her neck. She appeared sophisticated in that simple French sort of way. Her dark hair was even in a chignon.

"Yes," Lizzie whispered.

We grabbed some food and quickly found some seats in the half circle of chairs in Lolly's snug, which was covered in cabbage rose wallpaper. It worked for her, like a contemporary grandma style. Mr. Poe curled up between us, but then lifted his head and shot me a give-me-some-treats look.

"No." Lizzie pointed a finger at him. "Stop begging. People food isn't healthy for you."

He huffed at her and put his head on his paws.

I didn't blame him. I wouldn't be crazy about humans restricting my diet either. Little dude loved food as much as I did.

"I've typed up notes for the agenda," Marianne said as she passed out sheets of paper. "We only have just under three weeks until the festival, and there is still so much to be done. But first, I would like to have a moment of silence for our dear Eva."

Everyone bowed their heads, and I joined.

After a minute, she cleared her throat. "Right, from what

Lolly said, the wake will be at the pub, date pending. The family is waiting on... well, whenever Eva will be returned to them. While we are all mourning, you know as well as I do that Eva would have wanted us to continue with our plans for the fête."

The others in the room agreed.

"She was a dedicated partner in our work, and she will be missed." She seemed to mean it all. Her voice even caught a bit at the end.

"Now, let's begin with our need for healthier food for our staff."

About halfway through the meeting, I found myself volunteered for two committees. One was the food committee with Rob. As a volunteer, I would make certain the booths were open on time, and that they were serving what they'd promised. I also had to taste test the food.

I mean, it was a tough job, but someone had to do it.

I thought it a bit weird that I was now the food police, but there could be worse things. I grinned. Only I could get a food-related job.

Brenna also quickly claimed me for the arts committee. There would be several booths, and my volunteer hours would be spent making sure that the artists, writers, and other creatives found their way from the green room, which would be set up at the pub, to their respective events.

I liked the idea of getting to know other creatives. Even though I wasn't exactly an extrovert, I missed hanging out with my writer and artist friends in New York. They were a mix of curmudgeonly odd fellows and supportive women. Out of all the things to miss since we moved, they were the biggest. Though we did keep up through email, it wasn't the same thing.

Kieran came in at about the half-hour mark and stood by the

dining table. Poor guy was probably starving. There were a few more reports, and then the meeting was adjourned.

"Please, do not leave me with all this food. Eat before you leave," Lolly ordered.

I leaned over to my sister. "I need to chat with Kieran. I'll be back in a minute."

She nodded.

When I was close to the table, he nodded toward the back door. I grabbed one of Lizzie's cookies and followed him outside.

"What's up? Did you get the ME's report back?"

"Hello, to you too," he said.

I laughed. "Sorry. You know I have a one-track mind. Hi, Kieran. Did you get the report back?"

He chuckled. "A partial one."

"And?"

"You have to promise to keep the news to yourself. Can you do that?"

I made a face. "You know Lizzie is going to ask and I don't want to lie to her. Rob and Brenna are already suspicious. They saw us walking out together. But I can swear it won't go beyond our little group."

He sighed.

I crossed my heart. It was childish, but my sister and I still did it. So, it had become a habit.

"What are you doing?" He gave me a look that spoke volumes. He thought I was nuts.

I cleared my throat. "Nothing. So? Was it murder?"

He nodded. "It appears so. There was insulin in her bloodstream. They are still running tests for other toxins. Like I said, only a partial report so far. But the influx of the drug caused a heart attack. Her body just couldn't keep up."

"But she's not diabetic, right? Last night her granddaughter didn't mention that. Someone dosed her with insulin and thought it wouldn't show up in the bloodstream. But that's a misconception. It can hang around for some time."

His eyebrows went up.

I shrugged. "I used it in one of my books. Was the bruise on her neck the point of entry?"

"Most likely," he said. "I asked you not to speak to anyone about it, but I have a feeling you've done exactly that."

"Um." I wasn't sure exactly what to say.

"Perhaps when you were at the garden center earlier?"

"How did you know?"

"Sheila saw you heading to the court with a wheelie full of plants."

I smirked. "Right. The police know all in this town."

He shrugged.

"We didn't learn much, except that maybe we should speak to Marianne. I was thinking maybe you and I could do that together tonight. And, in my defense, I was buying my sister some gifts."

He shook his head. "Too many ears and eyes around tonight. The last thing we want is for the killer to know we suspect something."

"Oh." I was disappointed but I understood his point. "And you think they might be here?"

He shrugged. "You know better than most, the killer is usually someone the victim knew."

"I feel so sorry for Mrs. Walsh. Part of me hoped it was just old age."

"I share your sentiment. This will be difficult for the family as well."

"And it means we have a new murderer running around town." I sighed.

"Won't be great publicity for the fête," he said. And then he held up a hand. "I know how that sounds. Once word gets out, there will be no putting that genie back in the bottle."

I smiled.

"What?" He gave me a strange look.

"That was a very American cliché you just used."

"You're rubbing off on me. Get it. Genie."

I laughed. "For the record, I would never use a cliché like that. It's writer 101."

"So, do you have a list of suspects in your notebook?" he asked.

"I've written a few names down. I did learn from Mr. McCormick that the deceased and Marianne had been arguing a great deal lately. And not just about the festival."

"Oh?"

I nodded. "She's first on my list."

When I opened the back door to go back inside, I jumped. Lizzie, Rob, and Brenna stood there so close that I nearly bumped into one of them. Then they turned away suspiciously.

Had they tried to listen into mine and Kieran's conversation?

I grinned. Mainly because it was something I would have done.

Kieran glanced at them and shook his head.

"How much did you hear?" I asked softly. They appeared to be the last three left in Lolly's house. I didn't realize we'd been outside for so long.

"Nothing," Lizzie said. "Lolly's place is airtight. Did he ask you out again?"

"What?" I nearly choked on the word. "No. Of course not. We were discussing the case."

"And?" Rob asked.

"Who else is here?"

"Just Lolly," Brenna said. "After helping to clean up, we were waiting for you." And they had just happened to have their ears to the door. Darn. Even though Kieran didn't want to corner Marianne in front of everyone, I'd planned to at least make conversation with her.

"Is it murder?" Lizzie asked. "Please say no." I could tell she really was hoping for that answer.

"I'm afraid that it is looking that way," Kieran said.

Their eyes went wide.

"Oh. No," Brenna said.

"Exactly, which is why I need you to keep that information to yourself. We do not want the killer to think we are onto them." He added, "Promise me that you'll keep your word."

"We promise," they said together.

"Was it someone at the bookstore?" Lizzie asked.

"It's a possibility, which is why I need you to keep an eye out. If you see or hear anything let me know."

"I can't believe someone killed Eva," Lolly said from the kitchen. "She had a mouth on her, but she wouldn't hurt a soul. We all have our quirks, and that was hers. And she was a lovely friend to me when your grandfather died." She came to the archway between the dining room and kitchen. She dabbed her nose with a handkerchief.

"I'm sorry, Gran," Kieran said, and it was obvious he meant it. He went over and hugged her. He was such a kind man and genuinely cared about people. I sometimes forgot that when we butted heads.

"Do you know if she was arguing with anyone?" I asked. "I mean, it could have seemed harmless at the time but maybe she angered the wrong person."

Lolly shook her head. "It would be easier to say who she wasn't arguing with in some way. Though, she wasn't the biggest fan of Jeremy, Clara's husband. Between his drinking and gambling, he'd caused poor Clara more worry than any woman deserves. I'd start there."

Except, Jeremy hadn't been at the bookstore. Kieran and I looked at one another, but at least he was a place to begin.

SIX

Before I'd even woken up the next morning, my sister had already planted her new fairy garden and left me a note with chocolate chip scones. In my defense, I'd been up late working on my next book. I hadn't been able to sleep after the meeting the night before.

I put two scones on a plate with the fresh whipped cream from the fridge, made my cortado, and headed to my office. I'd been writing for an hour and a half or so, when my phone dinged. Normally, I'd have left it in the other room while I wrote but I had no willpower when we were in the middle of a case, and I constantly wanted to check things out that I thought about. I had turned the internet off on my computer, but I'd forgotten my other addiction—my phone.

"I'm finishing this chapter," I said to Mr. Poe. "And nothing can stop me."

My phone dinged again.

I pursed my lips. My train of thought was gone anyway.

"Well, that lasted five minutes."

The text read: *Emergency food committee meeting pub lunch. Marianne will be there.* It was from Lizzie.

Ugh. I knew I shouldn't have volunteered. I wanted to text an excuse. But that second sentence about Marianne made it impossible. The leader of the committees had left quickly after the meeting the night before and I didn't have a chance to say hello—or question her.

While she wasn't a likely suspect, she was well connected. My sister, Rob, and Brenna had all said that, like Lolly, Marianne knew what was going on with everyone in town. She was closer to mine and Lizzie's age, and it never hurt to make a new friend.

That, and I wouldn't disappoint Rob and Lizzie. I'd volunteered for their committees, so I had to follow through on my obligations. I didn't want anyone thinking I was a snob or that my time was more precious than theirs. It wasn't.

After I saved my document, I took my coffee mug to the kitchen to rinse it out. Mr. Poe barked.

"We're about to go on a walk, but go ahead," I said. I opened the back door for him.

He took off toward the back gate.

Is someone there?

He wouldn't stop barking. I walked back there to see, but no one was there. He growled, which he seldom did.

"What is it, boy?"

The sky was gray and threatened rain. I glanced down the back path, but I didn't see anyone. His growling stopped.

Had someone been watching the house? I didn't like the idea that was still happening. There had been several times before my book tour when my sister and I felt like someone might be watching us. But we put it down to living in a small town, where everyone did keep an eye on one another.

Still, I shivered.

I needed to check with Kieran about those cameras on the footpath behind our houses. They were supposed to set them up when I was gone. We'd had a few incidents on the back path that went from the castle up on the hill down to the sea. The beautiful rocky road went behind our homes on the court, and past the town, all the way down to the boat dock and cliffs.

I shook it off.

"Come on, boy. We need to get to the pub." At the mention of the pub, which held some of his favorite foods and was open to dogs, he ran past me and back to the house.

I grinned. He was such a smart little dude.

I glanced back, and then decided maybe it was an animal or some birds. Mr. Poe was not a fan of any sort of intruder. He barked at squirrels and birds, but he had a different bark for humans. It was slightly sharper and that's what I'd heard.

A few minutes later, we'd walked down to the Crown and Clover. It was only eleven in the morning, a bit early for the locals' lunch, so there weren't many customers. Matt, the owner, had an armful of glasses, and motioned with his head. "They're at your table."

"Thanks." I grinned. I liked the idea we had a special table at the pub. It made me feel like we'd really become a part of Shamrock Cove.

Lizzie was at our table in the back corner, which had another table attached to it. Mr. Poe headed around to my sister for his dose of adulation from her. Bernard was laid out at Lolly's feet, and I sat down beside her.

"Here she is," Lizzie said.

"Apologies if I'm late. I was writing, and I always lose track of time. Did I miss anything?" I smiled at Marianne, hoping to get on her good side.

"Just in time, luv," Lolly said. "The pub is providing food for our volunteers during the festival, and we're here to try out some of the options."

"I'm always up for a meal," I said.

"They are also providing a green room for the volunteers in

the back of the pub," Lolly said. That was where they held most of the town's indoor celebrations from parties to wakes.

"We want to make certain it is nutritious and isn't going to make them tired," Marianne said primly.

And they wanted pub fare? I didn't say it out loud, a look from my sister squelched that question before it reached my throat. I loved the food here, but it was far from healthy.

A cup of coffee was sitting in front of me, and I hadn't even seen Matt put it down. But we'd been coming here long enough that he knew my favorite drink whether it was morning or night.

"Thank you," I said.

"Always welcome," he said. He picked up some of the other cups on the table. "I'll be back with more and the first tray of food from Ma."

Marianne nodded and smiled at him. "That is kind of you, thanks."

I was still very confused as to why we were here. "I would have thought we were well aware of all the pub food," I said. "And we know it's all delicious."

"I think I mentioned that they have some new ideas for the event," Rob said. "Matt wanted us to pick and choose what we want. And it will be a bit of a test, as they will add some of the favorites to their regular menu. He's been working on healthier versions of pub food."

That seemed a shame, but I didn't say it out loud.

"Not to change the subject, but I was curious if anyone had spoken to Clara," I asked. "Are they doing okay? Is there something we can do for them?"

My sister tried to suppress a smile. She was well aware of what I was doing.

"I spoke with Clara this morning," Lolly said. "She's never had to plan a wake and funeral, and I offered to help with the arrangements."

"As did I," Marianne added. "We're meeting with the

family and the funeral director later on this afternoon. Eva deserves a proper send-off for a woman of her stature. She was well loved in this town, and we will make certain she receives what she deserves."

It was the way she said that last bit that set alarm bells off in my head. There was a harshness in her tone. *What she deserves...* Hmm.

As if she realized it, she made the sign of the cross. "Bless her soul," she said softly.

What was that about?

"Here are the crudities and canapés," Matt said, as he placed two giant trays of veggies cut into flowers along with appetizers of all sorts.

"It all looks wonderful," Lizzie said.

"I agree," Rob countered. "Our volunteers may never leave."

"Oh, that's just the beginning," Matt said. He wore a huge grin. "Ma has gone all out."

He didn't lie. For the next hour and a half, he plied us with all kinds of food. Some Irish favorites in healthier, but just as tasty, versions. Mixed in with hummus and other things from around the world.

"Someone will have to roll me back up the hill," I said.

"Same." My sister laughed.

"I have another meeting in a few minutes at the church," Marianne said. "I need to go. But I think we are all agreed on our favorites. Rob, will you let Matt know? And tell him and his mother thank you."

"I'll take care of it," Rob said.

"I'll walk up the hill with you," I said to Marianne.

She frowned but then nodded.

"I'll take Mr. Poe with me," Lizzie said. "You go on."

As we left, I opened the door for Marianne.

"Thank you," she said tightly. "I suppose you want to interrogate me about poor Eva."

Before I could answer, she waved a hand. "I've been expecting it. I suppose Kieran will be asking as well. Did we always get along? No. She was as stubborn as they come, and she seemed to like adding drama to any situation."

I was surprised. This was quite different from the way she'd been the night before.

"We did have some cross words over the years. Mainly, because she often lacked any sort of decorum and liked to rub people up the wrong way, as you Yanks say."

"I see."

"I didn't kill her though. If I had, it would have been long ago when she was spreading rumors about my late husband, Griffin. Of course, she did it after he died so he couldn't defend himself. She was full of mischief and jealous, I think, of anyone who had a healthy relationship."

"I'm sorry for your loss," I said.

"Thank you. I miss him. And I hated that she sullied his memory with her lies. He did travel a great deal, but he did not have a woman in every port. I have no idea why she spewed such lies."

"May I ask when and how he passed?"

She stopped and blew out a breath. "Several years ago. His death was sudden. A heart attack," she said.

That seemed odd, since the same sort of thing may have happened to Eva. Though it was brought on by the insulin.

"Did he have any other health issues?"

"He was a diabetic," she said.

I nearly tripped on my feet. Could she have used his left-over medicines to poison the dead woman?

"The disease, especially with men, can be quite stressful on the heart," she said sadly. "When I was younger, I was a nurse. I never could make him eat healthy food. He was in a hotel room in Edinburgh when it happened. The police thought someone else might have been in the room with him."

She paused again and sniffed. "That's how the rumors began. But I asked the police point blank if he'd had an affair."

"That must have been awful for you. Had you suspected something?"

"Only when they said someone else had been in the room. But the bed hadn't been slept in, and they didn't think it was any more than his lifestyle catching up with him. Like I said, he refused to take care of himself. He liked his drink and food and wasn't willing to give up either. My guess, he was conducting business with the other person. He must have died after they left.

"So, if you're wondering if I had motive to kill poor Eva for spreading rumors, perhaps. In a weak moment, I spoke my worst fears aloud to her all those years ago. I thought she was my friend. It hurt what she did. But why kill her? Her health was failing, and it isn't healthy to hold onto hurt. I couldn't continue on with the anger. And the police never found any evidence my husband was cheating.

"I was quite determined to make her understand how much her lies hurt me. I said I'd press charges if she continued to spew her vile assumptions, and she stopped. She even apologized. Her husband was a bit of a dandy, and she had a habit of judging all men by his actions. And that was that. We ended up becoming dear friends. Once she told me about her husband, I felt sorry for her."

"Well, at least she admitted she was wrong."

"Exactly, which is why I had no reason to kill her. I am curious, though. Perhaps you'd like to answer a question for me?"

"If I can," I said.

"If you're asking me so many questions, does that mean her death is suspicious? Because, if it is, I can point you toward several other people she has offended over the years. I make her sound terrible, she wasn't. But she seemed to like the idea that other people were just as miserable as she."

"It's an ongoing investigation," I said. "I'm just curious about her. She died at my signing, and I feel this weird sense of responsibility toward her." That was true. I'd found her. "I understand that she was outspoken, but did she really have enemies? You seem to think so."

"Oh, my dear, so many. There would be a list. If you give me some time, I'll make one up for you. At least, the people I know about. You are correct, she was outspoken, but often to her detriment. She tried to make others feel small to make herself feel better. Sad, really, when you think about it. I tried to be kind to her and, after our chat years ago, she never said another thing about me. I can't say that about some others in town. Though I can't imagine anyone wanting to hurt her. She was harmless."

She wasn't wrong. I'd known people through the years who were the same way. They said hurtful things because they were stuck in a state of self-hate and sadness.

"But so many people say she was kind, and her family seems to adore her."

She paused when I said that. Her sunglasses covered half her face, so I couldn't read her.

"None of us wants to think badly about our family. And you haven't lived here long, but we normally do not speak ill of the dead. It doesn't matter how awful they might have been in life."

Interesting, again, how she said awful.

But more suspects were not good news, especially if Kieran wanted to tie up the case before the fête.

SEVEN

I should have gone home and resumed writing, but I wanted to share with Kieran what I'd learned. I had no idea if he was at the station, but I headed that way. While Marianne climbed the hill to the church, I crossed the street.

Inside the quaint cottage that was the station, Sheila was at the front desk. "Hello, traveler, how was the tour? I wanted to ask you the other day, but you know how Kieran is about murder scenes. Likes it all profesh."

"I do understand. It was fun, in an exhausting way. But you won't hear complaints from me. I'm so grateful that people actually stand in line to get their books signed."

"It sounds so worldly and fun, being famous."

I laughed. "I guess maybe from the outside looking in, but I don't see myself that way. I'm just grateful to the readers for showing up."

"I always say you have your head on straight."

I smiled. "Thank you, Sheila. Is he in?"

"He is. Let me see if he's off the phone with Dublin." She pushed a couple of buttons. "Your favorite writer is here. Are you available?"

I couldn't hear his side of the conversation.

She nodded toward me. "Head on back."

"Thanks."

When I opened the door, he stuffed some chips in his face, or French fries as we called them in the States. He waved me in. "Sorry, been on the phone for an hour with the boss. I haven't had lunch yet."

"No problem. I already ate at the pub. The food committee had a meeting there. You can eat while I tell you about Marianne."

He sighed. "I told you not to interview suspects without me."

"It was a chat as we walked up the hill, not an interview. In fact, she started telling me everything before I could even get a question in."

"That sounds like Marianne."

I reiterated everything she'd said.

He frowned. "I'd forgotten about the husband."

"Weird, right? That he died from diabetes complications, and then our victim had insulin in her system."

"It is strange. You think she might have used some leftover medications on her friend? I've known Marianne a long time. She was a few years ahead of me in school. She's bossy and gets things done, but I can't see her killing someone, especially a friend."

"I'm not certain how friendly they were," I said. "As we know, Eva was a bit of a gossip. They had some words over Marianne's husband years ago because of Eva's tale-telling."

He grimaced and then shook his head. "You know how it is here, Mercy. And Eva and my grandmother are from a different age before everyone shared their lives on social media. I'm not saying it is right, but it is how they learned about one another and what was going on in town."

I nodded. "I do understand, more than you think. But our

victim had spread some not-so nice rumors about Marianne's dead husband. As in, she insinuated there was an affair involved."

He sighed, as if he were more interested in facts than gossip.

"I'm only sharing the information she provided."

He nodded. "Go ahead."

"Eva spread rumors that the husband hadn't been alone in the hotel room where he was found, and that he died suspiciously. Though Marianne swears they discussed it and moved past it, I'm not certain if that is true. That is pretty damaging, especially when someone is mourning. And if it wasn't true, it's just mean. That and there was an edge in her voice that didn't quite mesh with the idea that she was over her hurt considering the matter."

"You're talking about a woman who is as well-respected as my grandmother in this town," he said. He grinned. "I can see those wheels of yours turning, but I can promise you she isn't a killer." He typed on his computer.

"What are you doing?"

"I'm looking up the case notes on her husband. I wasn't here when all of that happened. The case was handled by the local authorities where he died.

"Let's see. The death was reported by the manager of the hotel. They had received a call at reception that someone was in distress. But the call had come from outside the hotel. The number couldn't be traced."

"Well, that's definitely suspicious. I mean, why wouldn't they search for the person with the number?"

"It belonged to a payphone. Do they even still have those? And you're right. Since he had previous health issues, including a cardiac event, it was deemed natural causes."

"Didn't they think it was odd the call came from a payphone?"

"Well, I would have, but they probably had tons of cases, and I'm sure this one appeared simple on the surface."

"What if Marianne killed him? Did they do an autopsy?"

"Let's not assume anything. A cursory one was done. He was over the legal limit of alcohol and had prescription meds in his system. All of which were confirmed by his doctor."

"What if this wasn't the first time the killer used too much insulin?"

He clicked a few more times. "That would have come up in the medical report. They did check alibis. Marianne was here at some garden party that night. That's where local authorities informed her what happened. According to the file, she was greatly distressed by the news. She completely broke down and had to be hospitalized. The detective noted he'd never seen her so bereft. She definitely wasn't any sort of suspect."

"Don't you think we should reopen that case?"

He chuckled. "It's not that easy, Mercy. We would need new evidence and there isn't any for that case. Though I will check with the medical examiner to see if she remembers anything and if it has any correlation to our current one."

I hid a smile with a cough. He'd said *our*. "Won't that make her mad?"

"I can just explain we are following up on a death that may or may not be related."

Well, at least there was that.

"Again, we can't jump to conclusions. This isn't one of your novels and we have no proof in this case that Marianne is in any way related to Eva's death."

He didn't say it to be mean. It was his way of reminding me to follow the evidence.

"Still feels strange to me," I said. "She's going to the top of my list. I don't care how much everyone likes her."

He laughed. "What is it you are always saying: You do you.

But she also has a strong alibi. She left the bookstore not long after you signed her books. No one seems to have even seen her with Eva. I've been going through the photos taken by the newspaper's photographer. We need proof otherwise to consider a suspect."

"Stop turning my own words against me."

"Anything else?"

I shrugged. "Did the medical examiner think the death was suspicious?"

"We still don't have the full report, but out of all the ailments she had, diabetes wasn't one of them. So, definitely suspicious. According to her doctor, her health had been failing for some time. He was surprised she hadn't been using her oxygen mask and tank. She had a portable one."

"Oh? Remember her granddaughter saying they'd had an argument about the oxygen? Eva thought it made her look old. So, she hadn't brought it with her." The woman was in her late seventies, but vanity didn't always know an age.

"I asked Gran about it earlier, and she said that sometimes Eva was a bit vain. Her words, not mine. She said that Eva only used her oxygen when she was quite bad off. She didn't like looking like an old crone. Again, her words, not mine."

I grinned.

"Did you find the tank at her home?"

He sighed.

"What?"

"We're still waiting on the warrants to come through for the house. Judge Werner is out on his boat. He should be back tomorrow."

The judge lived in the next town over but dealt with criminal, and civic, cases for several of the villages nearby. He was old school, and insisted that if anyone was troubled, the police needed evidence to support their cause.

While Kieran would never say it out loud, Judge Werner had become the bane of his existence.

"Won't Clara just let you search? She seems nice enough. Certainly, she would want to know if someone killed her grandmother?"

"She agreed at first, and then her husband, Jeremy, came home and tossed out Sheila and the team. He said if we wanted to invade his home, that we'd have to go by the book."

"Well, that seems suspicious."

"He's a knobhead."

I laughed hard at that.

"It sounds like there is some history there."

"He's been a resident here at the jail more than once for drunk and disorderly. And he's gambled away their savings. That's why they were living with Clara's grandmother. Lolly told me that Eva had nothing nice to say about him."

"Oh. I thought they moved in to take care of her," I said.

"That's what they said to save face. Poor Clara had no choice if she wanted to keep a roof over her family's heads."

Well, that was news. "Do you suspect him?" I waved a hand. "Never mind. You always need evidence."

"You're learning. But no. Like I said, he's a knob but I can't see him being bright enough to commit murder. This one seems a bit sophisticated. Though I suppose anyone can learn something on the internet."

I laughed. "That's kind of mean. He seemed protective of Clara while we were there."

"An act," he said. "He's known for—"

"What?"

"He's not always been faithful to her and doesn't bother hiding it. I think it was part of the reason why Mrs. Walsh tried to redirect the attention of others. If they were focused on each other, then they would leave her family alone. Of course, I didn't find any of this out until Lolly came clean last night. Except for his drinking, I thought he was an okay bloke."

An idea formed in my head. Maybe the police couldn't snoop around Clara's, but I could.

"Whatever you're thinking about, the answer is no. Do not go and investigate on your own. You've done enough just talking to Marianne. She'll probably put in a complaint."

"She won't," I said. "She volunteered everything. Like I said, she started talking before I even asked a question. And she knows you'll need to question her as well."

"We'll see. She's on the police committee. I don't like to make her angry."

"What? Like she would threaten your job?"

He shrugged again. "She could. Please be careful around her and the group she hangs out with. They pretty much run the town. Well, with the exception of my grandmother, who is a saint."

"I'll keep that in mind," I said. "And I agree about Lolly. When I grow up, I want to be like her." I smiled. "She's one of the kindest human beings I've ever met, but she also has a way of putting people in their place."

An idea was already forming though. I just needed to talk with my sister. "Any idea when the body will be returned to the family? I know they were trying to put together a wake and a funeral. For some reason everyone thought I might know."

"ME said in another forty-eight hours. Takes a bit longer when there is a suspicious death. But you can relay the information if you like. I called Clara and left a message, but she hasn't rung me back."

I stood. "Thanks for sharing."

"Mercy?"

"Yes?"

"Please, be careful. I can see the wheels turning in your brain."

I grinned. "I have no idea what you're talking about."

He chuckled.

As I left the police station, my phone dinged. It was a text from Lizzie.

Need you at the store.

I wonder what that is about.

EIGHT

On the short walk to the bookstore, my stomach tightened with nerves. It was silly. She was probably busy and needed me to take Mr. Poe out for a walk. A few minutes later, I opened the door.

I was relieved to see she and Caro were busy at the counter with a line of customers. For a weekday afternoon, that sort of business was welcome. She held up a hand and mouthed five minutes. I nodded. Then I headed to the back to the small breakroom she'd set up in the hidden room under the staircase. Part of it was used for storage. The other part had a small fridge, table with two chairs, a coffee maker, and an electric tea kettle. The teas and coffee were in small book crates hung on the wall. It was later in the afternoon, so I decided on an herbal tea.

There were always cookies and cakes of some kind back here, and today it was snickerdoodles. My sister and Caro were big bakers, and they loved trying each other's recipes. I took one, knowing she wouldn't mind.

I'd just about finished when Lizzie headed back with Mr. Poe. She had stacks of papers in her hand.

"What's up?" I asked. She put the pile of papers on the table.

"These are for the literary contest. Remember, you agreed to be the judge."

"Is it part of my duties that I volunteered for last night?"

She shook her head. "This was from several months ago—before you left on tour."

I had no recollection, but I'd also been on a deadline before I left—a tight one. I'd probably said yes without really listening.

"*Okaaay.*"

"You don't remember, do you?" Her eyebrows went up.

"I don't, but I will do it. Are there instructions?"

"Yes. You're one of three judges, but your opinion counts for fifty percent of the total. Each of the sample chapters comes with a sheet for you to fill out and tally. Just remember, they are amateurs. Lolly says we need to be encouraging. You, me, and Caro are the judges. But we're not to discuss them. And Lolly will do the final tallying, as she is the head of the committee."

"Seems simple enough. How long do I have?"

She made a face.

"What?"

"You only have three days. To be honest, Caro and I did ours when they came in a month ago, and I just forgot that we still needed yours until Lolly mentioned it this afternoon."

That wasn't like my sister. She never forgot anything. I envied her brain for that reason.

"No worries. I'm a fast reader."

"I know you're writing, but it couldn't be helped."

"Don't worry about it. I actually have a favor to ask you."

She frowned. "Why am I always nervous when you say that now?"

I laughed. "It's not *that* bad."

"That's code for you need my help for snooping."

"I'm so proud. You really are catching on, but I think this is one of those times we can combine snooping with doing something really kind."

She sighed. "Okay, what is it?"

"You know how Lolly's group goes to the homes of those who are mourning and help to tidy up."

"Yes," she said guardedly.

"Any chance you're doing that at Clara's house?"

"Actually, yes. Later this afternoon. Why?"

"I need to look around Eva's room. They won't let the police in until the warrants come through. And that might be a couple of days, depending on when the judge comes back from his fishing trip."

She frowned again.

"What?" I asked.

"Clara doesn't seem like the sort of person who would mind the police. She desperately wants to know what happened to her grandmother."

"It wasn't her, it was the husband, Jeremy. Do you know anything about him?"

She shook her head. "He seemed caring that night we were there."

"You and I know appearances can be deceiving."

"True. If I put you on the cleaning crew, you *actually* have to clean."

"I will. I promise."

She gave me the eye again but nodded.

Her watch buzzed, and she glanced at it. "Caro needs my help. I'll text Lolly and tell her you are helping. Just don't forget the contest."

"I won't."

What was Jeremy hiding? And had he killed Clara's grandmother for control of the house and business? People murdered for all kinds of greedy reasons, and, usually, the killer was someone the victim knew.

. . .

A few hours later, we were at Clara's house. She and the family had been treated to a late lunch at the pub, thanks to Lolly's group of hens, as she called them. Meanwhile, the rest of us had gathered for our assignments.

I had Eva's room, thanks to my sister's chart list. She had Clara and Jeremy's bedroom. She'd promised to keep her eyes open to anything unusual. But said she wouldn't go out of her way to snoop.

I, on the other hand, planned to go through every single bit of Eva's room.

When I opened the door, a few bits of dust stirred. It didn't appear anyone had been in here in the last few days. There was a light bit of dust on all the furniture. I did as I'd been told and cleaned first. Then I quietly went through the dresser and her vanity.

I did feel a small twinge of guilt as I went through her clothes and personal items. The bedside table was filled with all kinds of prescriptions. I took pictures of everything with my phone. I thought I might check to see if mixing any of her regular meds with the insulin might have made the attack worse.

For someone whose health was failing, she'd seemed full of life. But the drugs told another story.

The oxygen tank was pushed against the wall. The tank showed that it was full, and the mask had an antiseptic smell as if it had been cleaned recently. Then I checked under the bed. There were a few boxes, but they were filled with winter clothing and coats.

I'd been hoping for some personal items. Other than the pictures on the wall, and a few knick-knacks, I hadn't found much. No letters or even bills.

Realizing I'd been snooping for some time, I headed out of

the room to find the vacuum cleaner.

I followed the sound of chatter to the kitchen.

"Poor, sweet Clara, do you think she has any idea what that husband of hers has been up to?"

There was a bit of tutting. "Shush, Hilda, they could come in at any time. We don't want to risk anyone overhearing. But I don't know what she will do if she finds out. He's a terrible sort. Acts one way around his family and then is out carousing to all hours. Surely, she knows by now. She's had to have heard the gossip. At the very least, Eva would have said something. She wasn't the type to let that sort of thing slide."

I wasn't surprised, as Kieran had said much the same. But it made me wonder if Jeremy might be a suspect. Had he killed his mother-in-law to get control of her money?

I cleared my throat as I entered the kitchen where several women cleaned, while two others loaded the fridge and freezer like a game of Tetris with more food than I was certain Clara's family could eat.

"Hi," I said. "I'm in search of the vacuum. Or hoover, as I think you call them here."

"Aren't you a sweetheart for volunteering," a woman said. "I'm Hilda and in charge of the kitchen crew. We met at your book signing the other night. Love the books, by the way."

"Thank you." I was probably blushing. I always did when people said nice things.

"I believe your sister has the hoover upstairs. Did you know the family well?"

She was prying as to why I'd volunteered so last-minute. All of these women had been at the book signing and had heard Eva's questions for me.

"I only met Clara the night her grandmother passed, but she seemed so kind. And I've talked to her kids at the grocery several times." I didn't mention I had no idea until that night the kids were Clara's. "This seemed like the easiest way to help out."

"Well, isn't that sweet of you," Hilda said. "For being so famous and busy, we are most grateful for your help. You and your sister have the kindest hearts."

I recognized some of the women from Lolly's group, but I was terrible with names. "I have to admit I heard you talking about her husband, which is a shame. I thought he seemed quite protective of Clara."

The women looked at one another. "Right, we shouldn't have been talking about that," Hilda said. "I—well, Clara is a sweet dear, as are her children. The husband—we can only hope he is supportive of her. I know her heart is broken."

"You don't think he would have hurt Mrs. Walsh, do you?" Darn. As soon as the words left my mouth, I regretted them.

There were gasps around the room.

"I bet she knows something," one of the women said. "She works with Lolly's Kieran. Was Eva murdered? We've been wondering since it's taking so long for the body to be returned to the family."

"I—uh, no. It's not like that. I write mysteries, as you all know. I guess I see everyone as a killer. And I think the medical examiner was a bit backed up. That's the last thing I heard. So far the police are just doing the regular sort of inquiries for a sudden death. Um. I should go find Lizzie. I'd like to finish up my part of this."

I turned away quickly but stood in the hallway for a few seconds.

"I knew it. She's been murdered," Hilda said. "Poor Eva. But who would do such a thing?"

"Hilda, you don't know that," another woman said. "And why? She was a busybody, but murder? I don't think so. Like she said, she's a writer. She's probably just curious since the death was so sudden."

"She is dating Kieran, and they spend a great deal of time together," Hilda said. "I promise you, she knows something. Eva wasn't harmless, but she offended everyone she met. You all know how she was." There was a long pause. "Bless her heart, though. She meant well. She just had a curious mind."

Yes. A curious mind that may have gotten her killed.

NINE

Once we returned home, we let Mr. Poe out. We didn't go many places without him, but it hadn't seemed right to take him out to Clara's while everyone was doing their best to clean and organize. Since we'd been in a van with the other women on the way back to town, we hadn't spoken much. But Lizzie appeared tense. I wondered if she'd found something.

"Okay, out with it," I said.

She cocked her head. "What do you mean?" She appeared genuinely confused.

"Something is bothering you. I can tell."

She blew out a breath. "I'm trying to make sense of it. To be honest, it's probably nothing."

"Share and maybe I can help."

"I overheard some of the women talking about Jeremy," she said. "They weren't saying very nice things. But he seemed so protective of Clara. I mean, it's weird that he's insisting that the police need warrants. But maybe that's more of him taking care of his family."

"But there is something that made you think the stories about him might be true?"

She nodded.

We sat down across from each other at the kitchen table.

"Out with it."

"When I gathered up the laundry, I found lipstick on the collars of some of his shirts."

"And? I mean, maybe it's Clara's?"

She shook her head. "I've never seen her wear any sort of makeup. Maybe a lip gloss. She has that perfect porcelain skin, pink bow lips, and long dark lashes. She doesn't need makeup. So, whose lipstick was on his collars? I hate the idea of him messing around on her."

"Me too. She seems genuinely kind, and her kids are amazing, which means she's a great mom."

Lizzie nodded. "If he is treating her badly... I just don't like it when women stay with awful men out of a sense of duty."

"Or she might feel like she doesn't have many options. She has two kids in college and two more that are high schoolers. She may need to rely on him financially. Though..."

"What?"

I scrunched up my face.

"Don't do that," she said. "You started to say something, finish it."

"I know that they moved in with Eva because Jeremy gambled away all their money. I don't know if they took out loans for the kids' living costs, but that's why they moved in with the grandmother. They also had to add staff to the store when the two oldest went off to university. If he's cheating on her as well..."

"Do you think she knows?" Lizzie asked. "I mean, sometimes it's easy to turn a blind eye when we don't like what we see. But she would have seen the lipstick. That is all kinds of wrong."

"It's hard to say. I've never had a successful romantic relationship with a man, so I can't judge. Though I would hope I'd never allow myself to be in a position where I'd let someone mistreat me. And you were lucky to have one of the greatest men either of us had ever met love you so dearly. But maybe he's good to her at home. At least, he seemed to be. Some women don't mind that sort of thing. For all we know, they might have an open marriage. Remember in book five of my series, the wife didn't care about the affairs, as long as he left her alone and bankrolled her shopping."

She frowned. "I do remember that. But Clara is a good soul and deserves better."

I smiled. "Remember, we aren't judging. But I do wonder if Eva found out about the other woman. I didn't know her well, but I couldn't imagine she would have stayed quiet about that."

"Do you think he killed her to keep her quiet?" Her eyes went wide. And we jumped when Mr. Poe scratched on the back door.

I stood to let him in. "When I asked Kieran about it, he didn't think..."

"You have to finish that sentence."

"If Eva was murdered, Kieran didn't think Jeremy was bright enough to plan something like that."

She grinned.

"What's so funny?"

"I just like Kieran's way of telling it like it is. He's a lot like his grandmother."

"That he is. At least, when he's willing to share the secrets."

"Does he have anyone in mind? I really don't like the idea the killer might be someone we know."

That was the worst part of living in such a small town. The killer usually was someone we knew, which made it all feel so much more personal for everyone who lived in Shamrock Cove.

"I thought it might be Marianne," I said.

My sister hooted with laughter. "Oh. No. You can't. Trust me. She might murder a pie chart, but she wouldn't hurt anyone. I've spent enough time with her to know that she wouldn't have anything to do with killing Eva."

"But there was some bad blood between them when Marianne's husband died years ago."

Lizzie snorted. "You said it: years ago. I watched them together. Other than rolling her eyes a few times, Marianne was always kind to Eva. Even when Eva was saying things she shouldn't. And, honestly, Marianne is so busy with all of her volunteer work, when would she plan a murder? I would put you up as a suspect before her." She laughed again.

"But her husband died from complications due to diabetes. And Eva was killed with insulin, or at least that's what the ME thinks so far. They are still running tests."

"Her husband died years ago, and she held on to his medicine just in case she might want to commit murder?" She snorted again.

"Well, when you put it like that," I said. "But that means we have to hunt for other suspects. If Kieran is right about Jeremy, that leaves us with no one on the list. Though the more I learn about him, the more I think Jeremy might be our man."

"Oh, I'm sure if we talk to some of the other women in Lolly's group we can come up with a few more," Lizzie added. "The art committee meets tomorrow. I can introduce you to a few of the women who were close friends with Eva."

"Okay, that sounds like a plan."

"If Jeremy and Eva didn't get along, it's possible he did kill her. Like you always say, people can look up anything on the internet."

"True. And I did say that to Kieran. He had a good point, though. Where did Jeremy get the drugs? If I remember the bruise, it went straight into the carotid artery. I feel like that took some kind of knowledge. But you could be right. Watch enough videos and you can learn anything."

. . .

Later that evening, I was in bed, but I couldn't go to sleep. Knowing I had a stack of competition entries to read on my desk, I rolled out of bed. After grabbing some herbal tea that my sister swore helped her sleep, I headed to my office and turned on the desk lamp.

Before delving into the first entry, I read the rules and looked over the evaluation sheet. It was fairly simple, and I was only asked to provide one brief comment about the work over-all. I remembered what my sister had said about being encouraging.

I also remembered some of my first contest entries from years ago where the judge wasn't so kind. I learned from those critiques, but it was also soul crushing in the same way that reviews could be of published books. It was hard to accept that my books might not be for everyone. I had to stop reading reviews for that reason. Better for me to live in a bubble with my characters than lose weeks of writing because someone was mean. Authors had to protect themselves and develop a thick skin.

The first book was from the point of view of a lamb. *Oh. My.* That said, it ended up being kind of funny the way the lamb saw humans as they went about their business on the farm.

The next one was about a woman finding herself on a cruise. I was fairly certain I'd read something similar, but the piece was well written. I judged each one as I read through the pages.

I was to the middle of the pile, when I landed on one that was a mystery. It started with a well-known woman in town being murdered. The woman had a habit of saying the wrong thing at the most inappropriate of times. As I read along, I'm sure my eyes grew bigger. This very much sounded like Eva's story. Then on the last page of the entry, there was a second murder of a man in town.

I checked the evaluation page, but there was only a number.

No name was given. Everything was anonymous so the judges couldn't show any kind of favoritism.

This has to be a coincidence.

But I couldn't shake the similarities. The woman was killed with poison, not insulin. Still, a shiver slid down my spine.

If this had been written by the killer, was there someone else already in the murderer's sights?

"Mercy!" My sister yelled so loud I jumped, and my chair rolled back. I almost fell out of it.

"Why are you yelling?" I complained.

"Did you stay up all night working?" She was like the work police with me, always insisting I sleep and take care of myself. Ever since our mom had died, she'd been a bit overprotective. If I was honest, I was the same way with her.

"Yes. But before you start nagging, I was reading the contest entries."

"Oh. Well, they could have waited until you had a decent night's rest."

"I couldn't sleep." I picked up the entry that I'd been curious about. "Is there any way to find out who wrote this submission? It's about a woman who wreaks revenge on townspeople who have done her wrong."

She shook her head. "Everything is numbered so all the judging is blind. Even Lolly won't know until we call out the number of the winner. That way everything is fair. Why? Is it good? I think I remember it."

"Well, yes. But it is also very close to Eva's murder. I was just curious. I mean, it could be a coincidence. Revenge is a popular trope for a lot of genres."

"Except you don't believe in those. Coincidences, that is."

I handed it to her. "Just glance at it and tell me what you think. You've read them all, right?"

"Yeah, but like I said, it was when they first came in." She focused on the pages. "Oh," she said when she turned to the third page. Then she glanced up at me. "Are you going to tell Kieran?"

I shrugged. "I don't think he'd take it seriously. But the second murder worries me." As I finished the sentence my phone buzzed. "Speak of the devil."

I pushed the speaker. "Kieran, what's up?" I asked.

"I planned on leaving you a message," he said. "I didn't think you'd be up this early."

My sister grinned.

"I'm up. What's going on? Did you get the ME's full report back?"

"No. This is about something else. By chance on your way home from Clara's last night, did you see Jeremy, her husband?"

Lizzie's hand went to her mouth and her eyes went wide.

"No. We cleared out before they came home. Why? Is he missing?"

"He is. The family left him at the pub when they headed home last night. Matt said he stayed an hour or so longer, and then left. We're pulling CCTV. Could be he's just sleeping it off somewhere. But Clara is worried, so I'm trying to find him to put her mind at ease."

"We didn't see him last night..."

"What is it?"

"There's something I need to show you."

"Did you find something at the house? I can't use it as evidence. It will be inadmissible. I'm still waiting on the warrants. Though if Jeremy really is missing, we may be able to get in with probable cause. That said, my hope is that he's really drunk somewhere. He's known for that sort of thing."

"If you can give me twenty minutes, I can meet you at the station. It isn't far from the house. It's something someone wrote, and it was very similar to the way Eva died. And it hints at a second murder at the end."

There was a long pause.

"Do you know who wrote it?"

"We don't. Though I'm hoping Lolly can help us. It's for a contest." I explained about the number system.

"It will have to wait. Do you think you and Lizzie could help us with the search party? My teams are already out, but we can use all the help we can get."

Lizzie nodded.

"Yes. We'll see you soon." I hung up.

"Do you think Jeremy is dead?"

I sighed. "I really hope not."

TEN

After meeting up at the police station we headed out with Kieran, who led a team of volunteers to the beach, jetty, and cliffs. We separated into pairs. Lizzie and I stuck together, well, with Mr. Poe. He'd become quite adept at finding people. Sometimes, after their demise, but we didn't talk about that perhaps being the case.

Kieran had made it clear that he was certain Jeremy was fine. His disappearance wasn't that unusual. After a bad night of gambling, he quite often had to sleep off his drink. The detective inspector's words, not mine. I prayed he was right.

"Why do you think he might be around here?" Lizzie asked.

Mr. Poe sniffed the air as if he understood his job.

"We have a witness from the poker game where Jeremy was last seen," Kieran said. "He said he saw him heading down toward the beach. With the beach huts still open, we thought we might find him holed up here. It's happened before."

I'd only seen inside some of the beach huts south of the cliffs. They were brightly colored, one-room spaces. Families used them to store beach items, and to change clothes. Sometimes they were used as shade away from the occasional sunny day here in Shamrock Cove. Like the home where we lived, the huts had been handed down for generations. It was nearly impossible to get one if it wasn't already in the family.

"Look for anything that appears unlocked or broken. I'm going to check the jetty and the booths up there."

With so many festivals this time of year, the summer booths weren't technically closed down until the first of November. During the celebrations, they housed all sorts of artists, crafters, and food.

"Is it wrong I hope we don't find anything? Poor Clara has been through enough. Or at the very least, that he's alive. I'm praying that story isn't becoming reality," Lizzie said.

"I'm right there with you," I said. "There's no reason we should find him. If Kieran's right, he could be holed up in one of the barns we saw on their property. But he has people checking on those as well as the family."

"Seems like the rumors might be true. It's selfish of him to make his family worry like this. Aren't they going through enough?" She slapped her hand across her mouth. "That was mean."

I shrugged. "It was true. It's just you, Mr. Poe, and me."

"Everybody deals with grief differently," she said. "I know that better than most."

"But was he really grieving? Or did he kill his mother-in-law. He's still my most likely suspect."

"Only he wasn't at the book signing."

"He didn't have to be. He could have administered the poison at any time. She might have been taking a nap. And then it took a bit to kick into her system." Though, everything I'd read said that a dose that big could have stopped her heart quickly.

"I hadn't thought about that," she said. "That also means anyone could have done it. But now that you say it, wouldn't she have felt it in her neck?"

"You would think, but she may have been asleep or distracted when it happened," I said. "From the research I've done, the new injectables have needles so tiny the user doesn't even feel it."

"Hmmm." She reached out and pulled on a lock of a cabin that was painted in pastel pink and white. It looked like a snow cone stand to me. "Seems locked up tight. Thank goodness."

I grinned. I didn't blame her. I hoped we didn't find him as well. If he was drunk, I'd rather not have to deal with him.

We'd reached the end of the first row of cabins, when Mr. Poe yanked at his leash. He growled.

Lizzie and I glanced at one another.

"Please, no," she whispered.

"Could be that some sort of animal is down here," I said. "Don't worry."

I let Mr. Poe guide me past the first row, to the second one. He started to whine as we reached a blue cabin. The lock was on the door, and it was closed. But our dog hopped around barking. Lizzie checked the lock, but it wasn't open.

"Why do you think he's so upset?"

"I don't know. I'm confused."

He pulled out of her hands and started digging under the building. The cabins were built up a few feet, to save them from the dampness when the tide was too high.

I knelt down and my breath caught.

"Mr. Poe. Stop," I said it loudly, and he did. He sat down and then glanced back at me.

"What is it?" she asked.

"There is something under the cabin," I said softly.

She reached down and pulled our dog away from the place where he'd been digging.

Crud. "Jeremy? Is that you? Are you okay?"

Silence. I bumped the bottom of the man's boot with my own. He didn't budge.

I dialed Kieran.

"What did you find?"

"A man, I think. He's at the end of the second row of cabins."

"What do you mean, you think?"

"He's in the sand under the house. I didn't want to pull him out. I think it's a man, because the shoes are a large size. But it is hard to tell."

"Don't touch anything. I'm on my way. And don't let anyone into the area. I'm up on the jetty, but I'll be right down."

It took him a few minutes to find us. Lizzie had moved several cabins down with Mr. Poe and they sat on a step. She gave him some water in the small plastic cup she carried for him in her bag.

Kieran bent down. Then he shook his head.

"Do you think it is him?"

"Hard to tell. He is facing away, but it looks like him. Right size and hair."

"Maybe he crawled under there drunk. He may just be passed out," I said hopefully.

He put a hand on the ankle of the man. I'd been too afraid of messing up the scene and hadn't even thought to do that. But part of me hoped he might still be alive, though he was terribly stiff.

Kieran shook his head. He pushed on his walkie-talkie. "Send the crime scene techs, and call the ME," he said.

"On it," Sheila's voice came across the machine.

"Let me guess, Mr. Poe found him?" Kieran asked.

"He did. I'm sorry."

"Don't be sorry, unless you killed him."

I shook my head. "No. No motive here. But it sounds like there are a lot of others who may have had one. He was a womanizer as you said, and he gambled. It's possible he made someone angry. Or maybe, someone found out he killed a poor woman who couldn't defend herself."

"We'll gather the evidence and go from there. Could be he drank himself to death. It has happened before."

Was it sad that I half hoped that was true? Then we wouldn't have to worry about another murder. But if he didn't—we were looking for someone who may have killed two people from the same family.

"Poor Clara and her kids," I whispered. No matter what had happened, she'd lost her husband and her kids, a father.

And I had no suspects in her grandmother's murder.

ELEVEN

As if she knew, Clara stood on the porch with two of her children beside her. They watched us drive up the dirt road to their cottage. When Kieran stepped out of the car, she would have dropped to her knees if it hadn't been for her children. They held her up, but they all cried.

My chest tightened, and Lizzie sniffed behind me.

"We can do this," I whispered.

"We have to," she said softly.

We climbed out of the SUV and Kieran was already guiding the family inside. I'd seen the older children in the grocery store the family owned during the summer, usually running the register. They'd seemed older then. Today, they appeared young and vulnerable. My heart hurt for them.

Off to the right, the two younger children headed our way from the big green barn. When they saw their mother dip down, they ran forward.

"Come on, Ma," the two boys said, as they put their arms around her shoulders and helped her inside.

Losing our mom had been one of the toughest things Lizzie

and I had ever endured. That, and then there was the death of Lizzie's fiancé and his daughter a few months later. It had been a year and we were still recovering.

"I'll make some tea," Lizzie said. Her voice squeaked a bit.

The oldest daughter—Niamh—started to follow, but Lizzie waved her away. "You stay with your mom," she said.

"Tell me," Clara said. "What happened?"

"Clara, there is no easy way to say this." Kieran cleared his throat. I didn't blame him. I had a tough time keeping it together as well. It was the children. Sure, they were older, but the sadness. The watery eyes—it was too much.

"Are you certain you want the wee ones here?" he asked gently.

"We aren't wee," the youngest boy—Caleb—said. "We want to hear the truth."

The others nodded, though Kingston, the older boy, handed each of his sisters a tissue. It was obvious from his sniffling that he needed one as well.

Kieran sat down across from them. I stood behind his chair willing strength into him. This had to be the toughest part of his job.

"We found Jeremy by one of the beach huts," he said. "Unfortunately, there was nothing to be done." He paused.

"Why is this happening?" Clara sobbed and put her face in her hands.

Quinn sobbed. Caleb wrapped his arms around her.

"It will be okay, Quinn." Caleb squeezed her tighter.

"Da is gone, it will never be okay," she countered.

He nodded in agreement.

"Did someone hurt him? Like Gran," Niamh asked. Tears streamed down her cheeks. "Is someone trying to kill us?"

"Niamh, let the detective inspector talk," Kingston said.

"I can't comment because it is an ongoing investigation,"

Kieran said. "We won't know for a few days if there was foul play involved."

That wasn't exactly true. It was doubtful Jeremy had stuffed himself under the beach hut, but I understood why Kieran wanted to keep the facts to himself. Rumor and hearsay could kill a case.

"I don't understand?" Clara cried. "How could this happen?" She sobbed again.

"I wish I had more answers for you," Kieran said. "We are working on it, and I'm so very sorry for your losses."

"Was it too much drinking?" Kingston asked.

"Kingston," his mother admonished.

He shrugged. "Mom, you knew Da. His liver was sure to go as much as he drank." He shook his head. "Don't get me wrong, he was good to us. He wasn't a mean drunk or anything, but he drank too much. It was bound to kill him one day. We need to be honest about that."

"Like I said, it will be a few days before the medical examiner's reports are in," Kieran said. "If you are up for it, I need to ask you all a few questions."

"I don't know how much more of this I can take," Clara sobbed.

Lizzie came in with the tea and set it on the coffee table. There were different types of biscuits on a plate. She poured each of them a cup. The oldest sister, Niamh, leaned over and put sugar and milk in for each of them, as if she had done it many times before.

"I'll keep the inquiries short and simple," Kieran said. "I know you were all in the pub last night. Can you tell me what time you left?"

Clara glanced at Kingston. She had to be so overwhelmed. "I can't remember," she said.

"It was around nine," Kingston said. "Da wanted to stay

with some of his friends a bit. He said he'd get a ride later. So, we left him there."

"He should have come home with the family," Clara said. "He might be alive if he'd just cared enough to be with us." She sobbed again.

"Niamh, take Mom to her room. I'll talk to the detective inspector," Kingston ordered.

Kieran held up a hand. "I don't want to have to come back. It's best if I speak to you all now, while things are fresh. I'm sorry, Clara. But I need to know what you did when you arrived home."

She blew out a breath. "I went to bed. The kids turned on the telly, but I needed some peace. When I woke up, I noticed the other side of the bed hadn't been slept in. Sometimes when he comes in late, he sleeps in here so he doesn't wake me up.

"But he wasn't here. Then I checked the barn. He wasn't out there either. So I woke the children. They helped me search the grounds before I called you. He sometimes passes out in odd places, but we couldn't find him." Tears flowed down her cheeks. "Please, don't judge him. He had his demons, but he was good to us."

"Except for losing all of your money, Ma," Kingston said roughly. It was obvious the oldest son saw through his father's charms.

"Stop," she said rigidly. "No one is perfect. But you will not speak ill of your father."

Kingston sighed, and then he nodded.

"So, you have no idea where he might have gone after you left the pub?"

They all shook their heads.

"Did he owe money? Or have you had disagreements with anyone?"

"No," Clara said. "At least, not as far as I know. When we— He promised he gave all that up when we moved into Gran's house. He promised." She sobbed again, and this time it didn't seem like she would stop any time soon.

Quinn stood and wrapped her arms around her mother.

"We'll leave you alone," Kieran said. "But if any of you think of anything that might help us with his movements after you left, please call me."

My sister and I followed him out, but, as we opened the car doors, Kingston came out.

"I didn't want to say this in front of Ma. She's right, she's had enough sadness for eons. But you need to know that Da hadn't stopped gambling. The guys he stayed with at the pub have poker games on one of the boats in the harbor. My guess is that was where Da went next.

"I'm mad at him. Ma obviously needed him, but he was self-ish. I mean..." He huffed. "Yes, he treated us well. But gambled away all of their savings. Including our university funds. My sister and I work hard to support ourselves while we're at uni. Nothing wrong with that, but you need to know the truth about him. Those men he hung out with are a bit rough. You under-stand what I'm saying? I'd look there first. No one here would have hurt him or Gran. We loved them."

And then, as if the weight of the world hit him all at once, his shoulders slumped, and his head hung.

Kieran moved toward him and then put a hand on his shoul-der. "If you need anything, you call. And I don't mean just about the case. We are all here for you and your family."

The young man nodded and then turned to go back inside.

Even my cold, black heart had been affected by the exchange. Kieran could be enormously kind.

On the drive home, we were quiet. As if we were all trying to sort out what we'd learned.

"Do you think the poker game is a possibility?" I asked as we came to the edge of town.

"Yes. I know who he's talking about. Though they are good

at hiding the sites of their games. We haven't been able to catch them. If they are out at sea, on a boat, that explains why."

"Is it organized crime?" I asked.

"No. Nothing like that. Just some blokes who all have gambling problems. None of them ever want to admit it. They lose. They get drunk, and that's usually how they end up in our jail."

"But maybe something went wrong last night," I said. "Someone might have cheated. There could have been angry words."

"All supposition," he said.

"Right. You need evidence."

"That's where the real detective work comes in, and please stay out of it," Kieran begged. "These men aren't necessarily bad, but they can be rough sorts. You do not need to be asking them questions. Me and my team will take care of it."

I held up my hands. "Fine. I can tell when I'm not wanted." Though I had an inside man who might be able to elaborate. And Kieran couldn't do anything about me talking to him.

After Kieran dropped Lizzie and me off at the bookstore, I stood on the sidewalk for a moment.

"Aren't you going to write?"

"Um. Yes. But right now, I really want some Irish stew."

She wagged her finger at me. "He said for you to leave the gamblers alone."

I held up my hands in surrender. "I have no desire to go back on my word with Kieran. I'm just super hungry."

"Right. I'd go with you, but I need to check on Caro and Mr. Poe."

"I really am going to eat some lunch. When I'm done, I promise to come pick up Mr. Poe. He can hang with me while I write."

She stared at me shrewdly.

I crossed my heart in our childish way. "I will not talk to the gamblers."

But I had every intention of talking to Matt and finding out everything he knew about them.

TWELVE

At the pub, I was surprised the place was so full. It was later in the afternoon, and it usually didn't pick up again after lunch until early evening for dinner. I sat down at the bar, while Matt waited on another table.

"Well, if it isn't my favorite author," he said when he came back around. "Let me guess, she wants an Irish stew, soda bread, and some of Mom's Guinness brownies."

"It's like you know me. I heard about the first two being available, but I'm super happy about the brownies too." They rivaled my mom's and were so soft and gooey.

He checked his watch. "Let me put in the order, and do you want a pint or coffee?"

"I have to write, so coffee," I said.

"Coming up."

He headed into the kitchen, and I heard him chatting with his mom. She was young, and their relationship reminded me of the one my sister and I had with our mother. She was very much a cards-on-the-table kind of person, but she loved us dearly. Before she died, she'd always said we'd grown up together.

Matt's mom had been a young mother as well, and she loved her son dearly.

He came back out and made me a cortado and then sat it in front of me. "How are things? Any word about Jeremy or his mother-in-law?" He'd lowered his voice for that last bit, but the pub went quiet around us.

"Uh. Nothing yet. From what I understand, the ME is still doing tests."

"But didn't you find them both?"

I cleared my throat. He didn't mean anything by it. I would have been curious as well. Who was I kidding? I was curious.

"Actually, I have some questions for you," I whispered.

He glanced around at the customers. "Oh, that's too bad," he said loudly. "I'd hoped you had news."

The rest of the customers went back to their conversations.

I laughed. "That was brilliant."

"I try. So, what do you need to know?"

"I heard that Jeremy liked to gamble."

His eyebrows went up.

"And what would I know about that?"

"You run a popular pub where he hung out with his mates."

He grinned. "You want to know who they are?"

"That and I also know you're a fan of poker, and quite good at the game. I wondered if you'd ever played with that group."

"That would be illegal, and you are best friends with the detective inspector." His eyebrows went up again.

I hadn't thought about that. "And you know, better than most, that I don't share everything with him. Besides, he has to know them already. I'm just curious if Jeremy had a falling out with any of them. Or did he owe anyone money?"

He nodded. "He was either a bad player or the unluckiest man I've ever met. As for owing money, I wouldn't know. The games I play have buy-ins for a certain amount."

"So, if you can't afford the buy-in, you can't play."

"Exactly. There's a first and second place with the pot. Winner gets seventy-five percent, second, twenty-five."

"Is it possible someone may have paid the buy-in for him? And they wanted their money back."

He shook his head. "You sound like it's a bunch of your American gangsters," he said. "It's not. The group changes week to week, though there are a few of us who play fairly often. It's a stress relief for me."

"You make it sound like you win often."

"I do. I learned to play when I was a kid."

"Barista, bartender, and professional gambler."

He shrugged. "I prefer professional poker player. With the buy-ins, it feels like a safe way to play. It's no different than someone paying to go to a movie and a dinner. It's entertainment, nothing more." That last part sounded like he was offended.

"Please, don't take offense. I've nothing against it at all. I may have played a bit in Vegas a few times—for research, of course."

He grinned. "Of course."

"I know that he was in trouble for gambling. They lost their house and had to move in with his grandmother-in-law. Since they died so close together, I wondered..."

"If maybe one of the gang did it?"

"Right."

"It wasn't around here where he got into trouble. That much I know. Our games are safe in that way, like I said. It was more likely his trips to Dublin that did him in. I couldn't tell you about that. I also didn't know about them having to move into Mrs. Walsh's home. He told us that she'd been ill, and that's why."

"That's the story I think they told everyone to save face."

"Just ask me what you really want to," he whispered, as we'd once again gathered the attention of those in the pub.

"Do you know of anyone who may have wanted him dead?" I whispered.

"Honestly, no. He wasn't the easiest guy to get along with, but he bragged a lot about his kids. I feel so sorry for that family. It's too much." He frowned.

"They are taking it hard. We were there this morning with Kieran. Those poor kids. It broke my heart."

"Jeremy wasn't the best of men, but his kids are a wonder. Bright and talented. It's a shame. Let me grab your food." He headed back into the kitchen.

It didn't sound like we were dealing with hardened gamblers. It was a weekly game among friends.

When he came back out, he put the food in front of me.

"I have one more question," I said.

"Okay. I'll answer if I can."

"Was there a game last night? Or can you tell me who he hung out with here at the pub. His family said they left him here. I thought that was weird. You would think he'd be taking care of his wife and kids."

Matt blew out a breath. "He wasn't a bad man," he said. "But he was selfish in that way. If he had a chance to hang with his mates, he did. Last night, he played darts for about an hour, but then he left. I made certain he wasn't driving. I gave Kieran the keys to his car; before the search when you found him I wondered how he was getting home. It's a fair walk to their farm. I figured he'd find somewhere to sleep it off."

"So, he didn't leave with anyone?"

He shook his head. "He was alone."

That didn't mean he didn't meet someone. Perhaps at the beach hut.

I dialed Kieran.

THIRTEEN

Kieran didn't answer, so I left him a message. I really had to get some writing done, so I headed home. My mind whirred with possibilities, and I was more than curious about what the ME had to say about Jeremy's death. A text popped up from my sister reminding me to pick up Mr. Poe, and that the results for the literary entries was due the next day.

Home it is.

After picking up Mr. Poe, we went back to the house. Since it had decided to pour buckets on us, I picked him up and carried him under the umbrella. It saved me having to clean his paws. At the front door, I held him up so he could glance over my shoulder, while I put the key into the lock.

He growled, and I turned around quickly. Only to see the secret door closing in the wall.

I stared at it for a few seconds.

"Was it one of the neighbors?" I asked him.

He growled again.

A shiver slid down my spine. "Let's get inside."

Once we were in, I locked the door quickly.

I put Mr. Poe down. He just sat and stared up at me.

"What? Was I supposed to chase after the person?"

He cocked his head.

"Yep. Nope. I get in trouble every time I do something like that. Besides, it was probably someone heading to the shops. You're just being dramatic."

He huffed and went toward his food bowl in the kitchen.

Well, I guess he told me off.

Had someone been there? Was it our stalker? I'd hoped since I'd been gone for so long that had ended. Once or twice on the tour I had the uncomfortable feeling I'd been followed, but I was never alone. Either a publicist or bookseller was with me at all times. Even for my trips from the hotel to the venues and they provided drivers at the airports and train stations to pick me up.

But I'd still, occasionally, feel uncomfortable. I put it all down to nerves. While I was grateful for all the attention, I was also terribly nervous before meeting with the public. Though, once I started the readings I was fine.

I grabbed the stack of papers I still had to look at. I picked them up and headed into my grandfather's library. With wall-to-wall bookcases and two round windows, it was my favorite room in the house.

I put the papers down on a table next to one of the cushy leather chairs. Then I headed back to the kitchen where Mr. Poe sat patiently at the back door.

"It's still raining," I said.

He grunted.

I shrugged. "Okay. I'll be here with the towel when you're done."

He pawed at the door, and I opened it for him. He ran out quickly. I waited dutifully for him to come back. Luckily, some of our trees provided a canopy. He'd get wet, but he wouldn't be soaked. Still, I grabbed the fluffy towel my sister kept by the back door for him.

One small yip, and I opened the door. He waited for me to pick him up. I dried him off and then hung up the towel. He followed me to the library and jumped up on the ottoman. We kept a blanket there just for him.

Even though I needed to move on, I took another look at the story where the mother-in-law and son-in-law were murdered. They were both killed by the wife and it was poison.

I couldn't imagine Clara doing anything like that. She was such a kind and tender soul. It was obvious she loved her grandmother and husband. That sort of grief couldn't have been faked.

It didn't mean the person who wrote the story had anything to do with our crimes. But it was too much of a coincidence for me. I wondered if Kieran had talked to his grandmother about finding the person who penned the story.

I decided to move on.

I'd nearly finished when Mr. Poe barked, but it was his happy sound. It meant my sister was home.

"Where are you?" she called from the hallway.

"In the library."

The door opened, and Mr. Poe leaped off the ottoman. She bent down and picked him up.

"I think he missed you," I said.

"It was good he came home with you. We were slammed at the store."

"On a weekday?"

"I know. The village council has some new tour buses coming in from a company in Dublin for a look at a 'quaint Irish town,'" she said, and made air quotes.

"Well, Shamrock Cove is definitely that."

"Agreed. The bakery and the bookstore are on their stop. Along with the pub and a few other stores."

"Well, that's good."

"Except there are thirty customers all at once. Don't get me wrong, we're happy for the business, but it gets a little crazy. And my interns have all returned to school.

"That reminds me. I had to order more of your books before I came home. When they come in, I need you to sign them. Somehow your name ended up on the tour brochure."

"Somehow?"

"Okay, when we filled out the paperwork I may have mentioned autographed books and author sightings, though not guaranteed."

"That's clever marketing."

She grinned. "Especially when I use your name. As I mentioned before, I sometimes forget how famous you are. You'll always be just my sister."

"And that will always be my favorite title. To be honest, I say it all the time but I don't think about how popular the books may or may not be. If I did, I wouldn't be able to write. But I'm happy to help you bring in business."

"Good, because I was hoping for the tour next week if you could just happen by the store."

"Of course. You know I'm always looking for excuses when I'm writing."

"Are you though? Writing?"

I blew out a breath. "I will. Soon. I finished filling out the paperwork for the literary contest today. I'm so curious who wrote that one story and it gave me an idea."

"Oh?"

"If it was scored higher by you and Caro, then it might win a prize. At the very least, we could give it an honorable mention. Then the winner would have to come up on stage to accept, right?"

"That is a good idea but it's almost a week until the contest. I sort of remember the story. If you think it warrants an award, we can talk to Lolly. I mean, everything is supposed to be beyond reproach, but if it helps catch a possible killer..."

"Now, you're thinking like me."

"That isn't such a bad thing. You are very clever."

I snorted.

"The worldwide star. To me you'll always be my bookish sister who doesn't like people."

I shook my head. "And to me, you will always be the smart and popular one."

We laughed.

"I nearly forgot—there's a special quiz night at the pub. I'm tired, but I promised the gang we would go. And Brenna will be there."

"But it's not Thursday, is it?" Thursday night was quiz night.

"I've been traveling and all the days still run together. I have notices on my phone when I have to be somewhere but other than that..."

"I can imagine. And you don't have to come if you're tired."

I shrugged. "I don't mind. Is Lolly going to be there?"

"Yes, with you, we'll have our full team for the first time in ages."

"You said it's a special quiz?"

"Yes. Town history mixed with Irish folklore. I've been reading up. It should be interesting at the very least."

"And informative. Though, I know very little about the subjects, but I'm in. How about you, Mr. Poe?"

He grumbled in her arms.

I checked my phone. Odd, it had been several hours, and Kieran still hadn't answered me.

Maybe, he's busy.

Later that evening, we sat at a table with our neighbors, well sans Scott, we forgot he was traveling for work.

"It's okay," Rob said. "He wouldn't be much of an asset when it comes to our subjects tonight."

"Mean," Brenna countered.

"Truth," Rob said. "If it had to do with *Star Trek* or other television and film shows, we would have lost without him. But he's not a big history buff. I've been studying up, though. And Lolly knows everything."

"Lizzie and I have been reading up on the history of the town," Brenna said. "We've been quizzing each other."

I had no idea that had been going on, but I was grateful my sister had such a wonderful support system while I was gone. We both did when it came to our neighbors. Even though we'd only been here a short time, we'd all gone through a lot together.

"I'm going to run and get some pints before it starts and maybe some chips. Everyone want another round?" I asked.

They nodded.

"We'll begin in fifteen minutes," Matt said over the loud-speaker. "And, yes, we have fresh chips."

I stood in a short line at the bar.

"Do you know if there will be a wake for Jeremy?" a man said in front of me. He spoke to another gentleman in front of him. They wore cardigans and work pants. One had black hair, the other was a redhead.

"Haven't heard," the red-headed man said. "Sad business, though. His wife and kids lost poor Eva, and now this."

"Yes, and I'll never get back the money he owed me," the dark-haired man said.

"Lewis, that is unkind."

"But true," Lewis said. "I loaned him that last bit at the game. He promised to make it right tonight. I've a good mind to go to the widow."

The other man frowned. "But you won't. Let it go, man."

Lewis sighed. "I suppose you're right. Isn't her fault he was a swindler. Plus, two wakes won't be cheap."

"I hear her gran had money, maybe she'll sell the farm. Will be a lot for a widow to care for, don't you think?"

Lewis shrugged. "I wonder if she knows Jeremy owed money around town. Maybe, someone finally put him to rights."

"Murder?" The red-headed man's eyebrows went up into his bangs. "Not around here. Most likely drank himself to death. Heard they found him passed out on the beach. Dead as they come. You still coming tonight?"

"I am prepared to win."

"We'll see about that," the red-headed man said.

They stopped talking when they made their orders.

I understood that Jeremy had been a gambler, but if he owed money to someone, that would give us some new suspects. Including Lewis.

"Earth to Mercy. Are you writing a book in your head?" Matt asked. I hadn't realized I was at the front of the line.

"Something like that." I put in our order.

"Have you been studying up for tonight?"

I laughed. "That would be a resounding no. I didn't even know about it until an hour ago. But I came to support the team, and it sounded fun. I never know where I might find inspiration for my books."

"Oh, that makes it all more exciting. I'll do my best tonight."

I grinned. "You always do. Can I ask you the names of the two men who were in front of me?"

He frowned. "Who? Lewis McGuilly and Sean Reagan?"

"Yes." I glanced behind me. "I'll have questions about them later," I whispered.

He nodded conspiratorially.

He put our order on a huge tray, and I carried it carefully to the table. I'd been a waitress while I had worked on my first and second books. I'd also bussed my fair share of tables.

After I took everything off the tray, I took it back to the bar.

Then I settled next to my sister and Mr. Poe.

"Okay, we begin in five minutes," Matt said again over the loudspeaker. "And don't forget, on Friday we'll have live music from the Murray Sisters."

There were cheers all around us.

"They must be good," I said.

"They are." Lizzie nodded. "They sing harmony and it's beautiful. They'll also be singing on the main stage for the fête."

"There's a stage?"

"Oh, yes. Up on the cliffs. It's not very big, but people are encouraged to bring their picnic baskets and set up on the ground. We have several groups, but I have to admit the Murray Sisters are my favorite. You'll probably hear all of them in one of the meetings. The arts committee is still trying to decide on the order of the musicians."

Oh. Yeah. "Cool." I kept forgetting I was on those committees. "Wait, wasn't there an art committee meeting today? Did I forget?"

"It was postponed. Half of us couldn't be there because of the tour bus."

"I bet Marianne wasn't happy about that."

Lizzie shrugged. "She didn't seem to mind when I spoke to her."

Someone laughed loudly to the left of us, and I turned to see it was Marianne. Some of the people at her table were on the committees she headed, at least from what I remembered. But she was quite obviously flirting with the man beside her.

He was handsome in a rugged sort of way. He had light-red hair and green eyes. I hadn't seen him before.

"Who is that?" I whispered.

"Oh, Pastor Mark. He's new at the church."

"Wouldn't that be a priest?"

She shook her head. "No, he's at the Lutheran church down the road. That's where Marianne works as the church secretary."

"Hmmm."

"What?" she asked.

"Is it me, or is she flirting?"

She grinned. "It is hard to tell with her. She laughs at everyone's jokes. I don't think she knows what humor really is."

"Oh?"

"I think it is her way of trying to make friends."

"She seems so..."

"Uptight?" My sister finished my sentence.

"Well, yes."

"She can be. But like all of us, there are different sides to her. There's nothing wrong with flirting a little. If that's what it is. Her husband died years ago."

"I'm not judging."

"Speaking of which." She cleared her throat as she motioned to the chair beside her.

"I barely made it," a man said as he sat next to her. "Sorry about that. We had a last-minute emergency involving a tree and a broken arm."

When he said the last bit, I recognized him. It was Dr. Mason from the hospital.

Did my sister have a date?

FOURTEEN

It turned out having Dr. Conor Mason as one of our teammates was a good thing, as he knew so many of the mythical answers to the trivia questions. He also seemed to be incredibly kind and completely besotted by my sister.

A lot more happened while I was gone than she told me.

I wasn't surprised, in regards to Lizzie. She was the most amazing human I knew. Perhaps I was partial since she was my sister, but I was quite obviously not the only one who thought so.

"A one-sentence answer," Matt said over the pub's speaker. "Who is the Slender Red Champion?"

Everyone looked at one another and shrugged.

"I think I know," Conor said. "But you'll have to forgive me if I'm wrong." Lolly was next to him, and he whispered something to her.

Her eyes went wide. "You may be right. I think I remember that."

He wrote on the tablet: The story of Morraha. And then he hit enter.

"We'll soon see," Brenna said. "I've never heard anything about either of those."

"My gran used to tell me all the folk tales," Conor said. "I thought she made some of them up, to be honest. But they are coming in handy tonight."

"It makes me want to read about them," I said. "Some of the stories so far have been fun."

"The Irish can always spin a good yarn," Lolly said.

"Hey ho, we have a winner. That last one did most of you in," Matt said. "Lolly's Lighthouse Gang, you are the winners."

There were whoops around our table, and groans from others around us.

"I can't believe we won," Lizzie said. "It's all due to you all. Even though I studied, I knew nothing. Like nothing."

"Neither did I," Brenna said. "And I grew up on a lot of the stories, but we were in Northern Ireland, and that definitely makes a difference."

"For some reason, if it involved food, I could remember." Rob laughed. "But Conor, you and Lolly are the only reason we won."

"I'm just grateful for the invite," he said.

"Well, you are officially part of the team," Lolly said. "We'll expect you every Thursday for our regular rounds."

Conor smiled. "Yes, ma'am. I'll make sure I have time off on the schedule."

My sister's cheeks were bright pink.

I hid my smile.

"You're a good one, Doc," Lolly said. "Now, I'm going to gather our prize. I'll be back."

Mr. Poe grumbled on the floor. "Uh, oh. I think someone is tired. We should be heading home," Lizzie said.

"Actually, I need to speak to Matt about something," I said. "But you two go on without me."

She frowned. "I don't like the idea of you walking home alone."

"I'll stay with her," Rob said. "She's going to do some snooping, and I feel left out."

Lizzie shook her head. "I don't think that is safe," she said.

"Snooping?" Conor said at the same time.

"Yeah, Mercy helps the local police with their cases," Brenna said.

"I thought you were a writer." Conor appeared very confused.

"She is. A famous one," Brenna added. "But she writes crime books and has an incredible insight. She's like a whiz kid."

"I'm neither of those things. And I only have a few questions for Matt. I'm not snooping," I said adamantly.

Okay, I was. And I never lied to my sister, but Matt was safe.

"If it's all right, I'd like to walk you home," Conor said to Lizzie.

Her cheeks went pink.

I loved this for her. She'd been so heartbroken last year when her fiancé and his daughter were killed in a terrible accident. I didn't know if she would ever date again, which would be a shame. She had an incredibly loving heart.

"Thank you," she said softly.

"I won't be far behind," I said.

"And I'll also stay with her," Brenna said. "I like the idea of being a bodyguard."

"Does she need one?" Poor Conor was definitely confused.

"You have no idea," my sister said. "She's always getting into some kind of trouble."

They laughed as they walked off with Mr. Poe.

I turned to Rob. "How long has that been going on?"

He grinned. "Not long. She started volunteering at the

hospital. She helps out entertaining the kids by reading books. They've been chatting. But I think this was their first date."

"Do you think she knows it was a date?" Like me, she could be somewhat clueless when it came to interest from males.

"Who knows?" Brenna said. "But he is kind and smart, obviously. She could do worse around here." She motioned toward a group at the back. It just so happened Lewis and Sean were at that table, and they were loud.

"Are you two sure you don't mind waiting with me? Honestly, I'll be fine on my own. It's not that far home."

They both held up a hand motioning stop. "We told Lizzie we would stay, and so we will. What do you need to speak to Matt about?" Rob asked.

I told them what I overheard while waiting at the bar.

"That sounds about right," Rob said. "Though some of the others in that crowd are a bit rough. They usually borrow a boat and play while out to sea to avoid the law."

"Interesting. How do you even know that?"

"I'm just going by hearsay," Rob said. "I'm not a gambler, so I haven't paid that much attention. But you hear things if you hang out in the pub long enough."

I grinned.

Four men stood up from the table and headed out of the pub. One of them was Mr. McCormick, from the garden center.

I wonder what that is about?

"I'm going to follow them," I whispered.

Rob and Brenna looked at one another. "But..."

"Okay. It's snooping. I didn't mean to lie. But I can talk to Matt anytime. Those guys look like they are up to something. Mr. McCormick seems like he's in charge."

"He does," Rob said. "I don't think it's some weird version of the garden club. Brenna, you stay with Lolly and help her home," Rob said.

"But I always miss out on the fun." She wasn't really

complaining; she said it with a smile. "Okay, but you have to tell me what happens."

"Deal," I said.

I grabbed my jacket, and Rob and I headed outside. The men were walking across to the cliffs which had stairs down to the boat docks.

"Do you think they are going to gamble now?" Rob questioned. "It's late."

"Probably, that's why. Less chance the police might see them. And maybe easier to avoid the town gossips at night."

"There is that. Are we really going to follow them?"

"Yes," I whispered. "I want to find out which boat they take. Or maybe they take different ones. This way, I can tell Kieran. And we know that Jeremy owed at least one of them money. What if things got out of hand?"

"Except dead men can't pay debts," Rob said. "I heard that on the telly the other night. A bunch of gangsters went after a gambler. They broke his arm and threatened to kill him, but the main guy said that line."

I grinned. "Except I don't think these guys are gangsters. More like locals who loaned him money. But I'm going to take some pictures for Kieran."

"In the dark?"

"I have a new app on my phone. Actually, Kieran told me about it."

"He did?"

"Yeah. When I was traveling I explained that I could only get out and sightsee at night. I basically saw everything from a car. But he told me about the app."

"So, you and the good detective inspector were talking while you were away?"

I cleared my throat. "Um. He was keeping me up on the local gossip."

"Riiiight." Rob laughed.

"Shhhh," I hushed him.

The men paused and looked around. I pulled Rob behind a parked car on the cliff.

The men headed down the metal stairs toward the docks.

We followed but at quite a distance. I didn't want to chance a run-in with any of them.

As they passed the guard shack, they waved. The guard came out and followed them.

"Wait, is he playing with them?" I whispered the question and took a few photos with my phone, even though they had CCTV down here. But I had no way of knowing if the guard may have turned it off.

"This is fun and scary at the same time," Rob said. "I don't want to get caught by those guys. I mean, I can hold my own. You don't grow up gay in Dublin without knowing how to fight, but I'd be outnumbered. Do you really know Krav Maga? Lizzie swears you could kill a guy if necessary."

I patted his shoulder. "This is as close as we're getting. Except, I want to get a picture of the boat. But I can do that once they are all on it." We'd made our way to the guard shack, which was dark. "And to answer your other question, I've been studying martial arts for the last decade. Though, since we moved here, I'm a bit rusty."

I'd planned to start my practice again when I came back from the tour. But things had been hectic.

The men were still walking down the dock, so we waited.

I was about to step around Rob, when there was a hand on my shoulder.

I jumped, and then my training kicked in...

FIFTEEN

Before I could swing around and knee my attacker, he twisted and pushed me against the guard shack. "It's me," Kieran said. "I'd rather you leave my parts where they are."

Rob stifled a laugh.

"It's not funny. You scared me to death," I whispered the words, but the anger was there.

"Well, if you weren't sneaking around involving yourself in things you shouldn't, I wouldn't have had to scare you. Care to explain what you're doing in the middle of our sting operation?"

"Sting?" I glanced around. Sheila was just next to him and there were a few others behind her.

"Are you trying to find the group of gamblers as well?"

"That's for me to know," he said. "I'll ask again. What are you doing here?"

"I don't suppose you want to play I'll tell you mine if you tell me yours?"

"No. I'd rather you just tell me what you're up to this time." It was those last two words that showed his frustration.

"Just tell him," Rob said. "Or I will. I don't want to anger our detective inspector."

I rolled my eyes. "It's not that big of a deal," I said.

"Which is why you're skulking around in the dark putting yourself in danger?"

"You sound like my sister."

"She is obviously a highly intelligent woman. Unlike someone else. Now, tell me why you are here putting your life in danger?"

He just insulted me. I probably deserved it. He was right and, from his face, obviously worried about me. I'd come out here with no weapons, not even my pepper spray or taser, which he didn't know about.

I cleared my throat. "Fine. No reason to be insulting. I overheard those men, I think it's Lewis and Sean, talking about how Jeremy owed one of them money. And that they were putting a game together tonight. Lewis said he might hit Clara up for the funds, and I couldn't tell if he was joking. I was following them and taking pictures for you. I'd planned to tell you."

"Well, now you have, and you can go. We're in the middle of an investigation, you can show yourself home."

I sighed. "I was just trying to help. By the way, Mr. McCormick was at my book signing. Funny that he is a part of both situations."

"Right. Understood. But you can trust me, Mercy. I've got this covered. Rob, can you take her home, please."

"It would be my pleasure."

Rob gently pulled on my arm. I reluctantly followed him up the stairs.

"I don't suppose you want to stay and watch what goes down?" I asked. "We could hide behind one of the cars in the parking lot."

"Or we could get out of here, and you ask Kieran all about it tomorrow. Besides, if we're too late, you know your sister will worry. Especially as she knows you are snooping. She just texted me."

I sighed for the umpteenth time that night. "Fine."

"Don't look so disappointed. You were obviously on the right track."

"How do you know that?"

"Why else would the police be here doing the same thing?"

"You make a good point. He better tell me about it tomorrow," I grumbled.

"You two are chatting about apps, I'm sure you can hit him up for anything you want." He nudged me.

"It's not like what you're thinking," I said. "We're just friends."

"Hmmm."

"What?"

"Well, you and I are dear friends and I think we maybe texted three or four times while you were gone. Sounds like it was a lot more with the detective."

"He's a source," I said. "You know, for my books."

"Uh. Huh." He laughed as we made our way on to Main Street.

We headed up the hill. I couldn't define my relationship with Kieran if I tried. Rob was right. We had talked a lot when I was gone. It had been easy and fun. But it had been kind of awkward since I returned home.

"Has he asked you out again?"

"I'm not talking about this with you," I said. "Do you think one of the gamblers killed Eva? And did they use the same device? That would be telling. Maybe they hit Eva up for payment. When she said no, they could have killed her to put the fear of God into Jeremy."

"Except he's dead as well," Rob said.

"True. This is one of those times where I feel like I've seen the answer, but I haven't quite put all the puzzle pieces together."

"Isn't that every case when you're in the middle of it?"

"Yes. I'm having trouble reconciling who would kill both victims. I can't believe Eva would have had anything to do with her son-in-law's gambling. Especially since the family had to move in with her. I mean, it's one thing if it's just her granddaughter, but there are four kids, two off at uni, and the husband. That's a lot."

"But she didn't seem to mind," Rob said. "Clara told me her gran liked having family around. She'd been lonely for years."

"When did Clara tell you that?"

"We chatted at my food truck a few weeks ago when the kids were all home. Eva didn't like the food, but the rest of the family loves it, especially Jeremy. She told me she was worried about her gran, when I asked about Eva. She said her health was much worse than they had thought. And that moving in had been a blessing."

"Did she say anything about the fact that they had to move in because of his gambling?"

He shook his head. "No. It sounded more like they were just helping out her gran. I mean, everyone knows Jeremy sometimes gets up to no good. But he seemed a decent father. I saw him around his kids. They joked around and laughed a lot."

"When you don't know someone, it's easy to pigeonhole them into one aspect of their lives," I said. "That's something I should know better than to do. People are made of many facets."

"That is true. As far as I could tell, and I didn't know him as well as I do Clara, he seemed a decent husband and father. Except, I guess, losing all their money. I can see why you'd think the way you do."

"When I create characters, they would be two-dimensional if we only saw them one way. I should know better."

He hooked his arm into mine. "None of us is perfect, Mercy. Real crime-solving is new to you. But you're good at it. Don't put yourself down."

I patted his hand. "Thank you, friend."

We'd reached the secret door, and he pulled me through.

"Okay, I've seen you home safely. Let me know if Kieran shares anything."

"Actually, I just thought of something. You said Jeremy was with his family at the food truck."

"Right."

"Have you ever seen him with anyone else? Besides his mates at the pub?"

"What do you mean, like another woman?"

I shrugged. "I'm just trying to widen my perspective of the man."

"By saying he cheats on his wife?"

"I'm going through different motives. Sex, greed... you know."

"Can't say I've seen him with anyone else. But..."

"What?"

"You said he was found down by the beach huts?"

"Yes?"

"Well, more than one of those huts is used for, um, liaisons. You know, out of the public eye. If someone were having an affair this time of year, that would be a decent spot to hide out."

Oh. My. Had he been down there with a lover?

Someone screamed.

Rob and I glanced at one another. "That sounds like Lizzie."

We took off for the house.

SIXTEEN

My heart thudded to my throat. *I'll kill anyone who hurts her.* Mr. Poe barked loudly. They weren't in the house, and we ran straight through the back door which was open.

"Lizzie," I screamed. "Are you okay?"

"I'm here," she said. But she didn't sound upset. "Sorry I screamed. I wanted to scare whoever it was. I didn't want them to hurt Mr. Poe. It worked. I think they've gone."

I ran toward the fence. She stood there with Mr. Poe in her arms. "He went berserk so I raced out here. I didn't see anyone, but I heard them running away. They may have just been on the path and we scared them to death. But I was worried they'd hurt Mr. Poe. He made a weird sound before he barked."

With a possible stalker on the loose, I took what she said seriously. "What kind of sound?"

"Like that time you accidentally stepped on his tail."

I'd felt horrible about that. I'd apologized profusely to our dog and my sister. He'd forgiven me the next day, but I was much more careful where I stepped in the dark after that.

"I hope the CCTV is working," I said. "Kieran is busy, but I will check with him in the morning."

"Oh, about the CCTV," Rob said. "The apple tree in Number One needs to be trimmed back. We've been waiting on the town council to get permission. We can't touch it until we do."

"Okay. I don't understand."

"It's blocking the CCTV camera on the path. At least, the one that covers the back of the houses on the court. They put it up when the trees were bare. I don't think they thought about what might happen when they bloomed."

"Well, maybe one of the other cameras caught something. I think we should get more for our home," I said. "And we need to leave it on when we are in the backyard. Anyone could be going down the path." I didn't like the idea of my sister, or Mr. Poe, being vulnerable.

"Well, that was enough excitement for a lifetime," Lizzie said. "Again, I'm sorry I scared you."

"You did the right thing. Though next time you're coming to Mr. Poe's defense, at least grab one of the pointy umbrellas."

She grinned as we headed back in the house. I double-checked the locks on the back door.

I tried not to think about our possible stalker. I had hoped he or she had gone away when I'd been traveling.

Maybe, they are back.

"I'm heading home. Though, I can sleep on your couch, or you can come over to mine if it will make you feel better."

"You're sweet, Rob," Lizzie said. "I probably blew it out of proportion. Whoever it might have been was obviously frightened by my banshee of a scream."

I made a note to call the security company tomorrow and make sure that I had cameras at every vantage point in the backyard. We had one camera that faced the back door, but I wanted more.

I let Rob out and locked the door.

"My nerves are jumbled," Lizzie said. "I'm making some

chamomile. Do you want some?" I'd grown to like the herbal teas she put together. She made them from the garden, and they just tasted better than the old tea bags we used in America.

"Sure." I grabbed the cookie jar and put it in the middle of the table. It was always full. Lizzie made sure of it. "Are you certain you are okay?"

She blew out a breath. "I'm fine. It was one of those reflex things. I heard Mr. Poe in distress, and I ran for him. I'm lucky it wasn't a bad person. Probably kids, and I scared them to death."

I picked Mr. Poe up and checked his paws. He seemed affronted, especially when I squeezed on his tail. He grumbled.

"He doesn't like that," she said.

"I'm just making sure there is nothing wrong with him. Maybe he stepped on a thistle."

She turned quickly and gasped. Her hand went to her chest.

"What?"

"Thistles in my garden? Mercy. That's just mean."

I put my hand in front of my mouth to hide my grin. "Sorry, I wasn't thinking. I only wondered why he yelped. So, how about Doctor Conor? He's a smart one, and he seems nice."

Her cheeks turned pink again, and she quickly turned away.

"He really helped the team tonight," she said softly.

"He did. No way we would have won without him. Though Lolly had the history of the town questions down pat."

"She did. I feel like I had a tutorial in the history and myths tonight."

"Same," I said. "I'm curious how the good doc ended up on our team."

There was a long pause. The hiss of the kettle the only sound.

She shrugged. "I can't remember how it came up. But I think I asked him."

"Was that when you were volunteering at the hospital? I didn't know you were doing that. Don't you worry about over-taxing yourself?"

"Oh, reading to the children is no bother. I enjoy it, and they seem to as well. It's one of my favorite things I do." That was my sweetheart of a sister in one.

"Have you been on a date with him?"

Another long pause.

"Uh. No. We've done some group things with our friends. You know, for the town. He's new here and didn't know many people. I've just been introducing him around, so he isn't lonely."

She fussed over pouring the tea and sat down, but she wouldn't meet my eyes.

"It's okay to like him," I said. "He seems kind of perfect, and you deserve to be happy."

She shook her head. "It's not like that. I mean, yes, he's all the things you've said. But I'm not ready to..."

"Date? It's been over a year."

Her eyes welled up.

I jumped up and went to hug her. "I'm sorry. I shouldn't have said anything."

She sniffed. "It's okay. But he was the love of my life. I can't explain it better than that. I'm not ready for anything new. Right now, the good doctor is a kind friend. Let's leave it at that."

"You are brilliant," I said.

"Why do you say that?"

"You're so aware of your feelings. Even sadness, I envy that you are so in tune with your emotions."

"Why do I feel like we aren't talking about me anymore? Let me guess, you ran into Kieran tonight while you were snooping."

"What—how? There's no way."

"Rob texted me when you almost killed Kieran. You need to be careful. Your body is a weapon."

"I'm actually a bit rusty. I mentioned that to Rob. I won't bore you with the details. All we did was follow some people and, of course, Kieran was already on it."

"And you will get the complete rundown tomorrow I bet."

"If he answers my texts. He didn't today. Which was why I felt the need to—"

"Snoop?"

"Yes."

She hugged me. "He is the detective inspector and is busy. You need to give him a break. Besides, what's to stop you from going straight to the station tomorrow morning?"

I grinned. "You are so much smarter than me."

She tugged on my ponytail. "Let me know how it goes tomorrow."

I moved back to my seat and sipped my tea.

She seemed reluctant to go upstairs. And then it dawned on me, she was still scared.

"Do you want to sleep in my bed tonight?"

"I—you're still jet-lagged. I can tell from the bags under your eyes."

"Uh. Thanks."

"I didn't mean it like that. I meant, it's a lot with me and Mr. Poe in your bed."

"Doesn't bother me. You know that." And it didn't. If she felt safer with me, I was okay with that.

I would do anything to protect my sister.

SEVENTEEN

After turning in my contest sheets to Lizzie at the bookstore and solidifying our plan to chat with Lolly about the one we thought might have been written by the killer, I headed to the police station.

While the rain had paused a bit, the weather had turned chilly. I put my hands in the pocket of my blue cardigan. I'd worn jeans and my black boots just in case Kieran wanted to include me in his investigations.

Doubtful. But I could be ready just the same.

Before I reached the door to the station, two men came out. They appeared exhausted.

"Don't know how I'll explain this one to the wife," one of the men said.

"I've got my story ready. I was assisting the police."

"Good one," the other guy said. "I'm worried about the fine. No telling what the judge will say. You know how he is about gambling. Though we might get lucky since he and McCormick are old friends."

"True. But it's a problem for another day. Let's head to the pub. I need to fortify myself before heading home. The wife is going to kill me. I'm sure she knows everything by now. Half the town probably does."

They passed by me. They smelled of cigars and whiskey.

It took me a minute, but I recognized them. They'd been in the group from the pub who had been headed to the boat.

I guess Kieran arrested them.

Sheila was at the front desk. She looked as tired as the guys who just left. I wondered if they were up all night.

"Is he busy?" I asked.

"Let me check," she said. She picked up the phone. "Sir, Mercy is here. Okay."

"He says go on back. He's been expecting you."

"Have you been up all night?" I asked her.

"We have. But I'm off in an hour. I'll sleep like the dead. And we caught those eejits last night. Kieran's being nice, offering release without bail for some of them, but after all the trouble they've given us, I'd lock them up and toss away the key. They are a blight on the village."

I adored Sheila. She always told it like it was. "Tell me how you really feel."

The second-in-charge laughed heartily. "Missed out on my beauty sleep. Always makes me cranky."

"I don't blame you."

She held up a hand. "And before you ask about the case from last night, you know what I have to say. That said, the boss will probably be happy to share with you. He usually is." She winked.

I waved and then went down the hallway to Kieran's office.

His door was shut, which was unusual. I knocked.

"Enter," he said sharply.

When I opened the door he glanced up from the pile of file folders in front of him.

"Hey," I said. "Do you have a few minutes?"

"Are you going to ask me about ongoing cases?"

"Yes." At least I was honest. "But you look exhausted. I know you've been up all night. I wanted to relay some information to you that I'm hoping will help you with the murder cases."

He motioned to the leather chairs in front of his desk.

"What do you know?"

"I think I mentioned the manuscript for the contest. The one that mentions two murders in thirty pages. Ones that are eerily similar to what you've been investigating." I had made copies for him and handed them over.

"You think this person killed our victims?" His look was incredulous. "I'll read it, but I would imagine it was a coincidence."

"Right. Except, I don't really believe in those. Perhaps it's someone's guilt coming forward. They wrote about it, and maybe, at the time, they hadn't been planning to see it through. It was fiction. But then what if something changed? The murders might have been a way of protecting the person. It's possible they forgot they wrote about it, or it was too late."

"That's a lot of what ifs," he said quietly. "It's been a long night, Mercy. And I have a suspect behind bars."

"Would that be Lewis?"

He nodded. "I expect you to keep that to yourself."

"I will, but you let his friends go and they are headed to the pub. I have a feeling it will be around town before the end of the day."

"You have a point."

"Why do you think it's Lewis? The whole dead men can't pay debts thing?" I said.

"It isn't about debts. Jeremy was a womanizer. Most in town knew that. Turns out he may have had... relations with the wrong woman. Namely, Lewis's wife. I've sent someone to pick her up."

"Oh. Well, that is news. You've been busy."

He gave me a tired grin.

"But why would he harm Mrs. Walsh? That doesn't make any sense. Any news about Mr. McCormick?"

"McCormick let them play on his boat for a price. That's as far as he went with that. He let them on the boat and then left the key for them to lock up. As for Lewis, he's not talking," he said. "No comment is his only answer. Asked for a lawyer, who won't be available until tomorrow. So, I'm going to the source."

"Do you think she'll say anything?"

"I can only ask. Why do you have that look?"

"I don't know the wife, or at least I don't think I do, but the crime seems sophisticated. Someone would have to know about how to use the drugs."

"You're assuming he died the same way."

"I watched when your men pulled him out from under the hut. He had the same sort of bruise on the back of his neck."

"The ME hasn't sent me the reports back, but I saw it as well. It's easy enough to look things up on the internet. Unfortunately, that is."

"It's one of my main sources for information, but I see your point. But the timing—and why kill Eva as well? That part of this doesn't make sense to me."

"You make a fair point, but I have to check."

"Understood."

"Do you have anything else for me?"

I shook my head. "I should go home and write. I'm several days behind."

"Good. That will keep you out of trouble."

"Except..."

"What?"

"If I go to the bakery and get your favorite treats, can I listen to the wife's interview?"

He rubbed the bridge of his nose. It was obvious he was

exhausted. "As long as your gift comes with coffee. Sheila made the brew this morning."

"Yikes. I'll bring a carafe." Sheila was a tea drinker and didn't really understand the fine steps it took to make the perfect cup of joe.

I laughed. "I'll be back in ten."

It was past the morning rush, and I had the bakery to myself. Well, almost. Lolly was at a table in the corner. Bernard, her faithful hound, was at her side. She appeared to have had one of her episodes and was sound asleep. Since he was her protector, it was best not to approach her when she was like that.

At the counter, I rang the bell. Paisley came out of the kitchen. "Oh, it's my favorite author. How was your trip? We missed you."

"And I missed you and your baked goods."

"Oh, I know you only love me for my chocolate croissants." She laughed.

"And so many of your other treats."

"You were traveling the world. I'm sure you had better, especially in Paris. Lizzie told me it was one of your stops."

I smiled. "It was, but I wasn't there long enough to sample the wares, which is why I'm here. I'd like two dozen pastries, a bit of everything. It's for the gang at the station. They've had a long night. And some of your coffee in a box."

"Oh, if you're headed back there, could you let Kieran know about Lolly. She usually snaps out of her spells quickly, but it's been almost an hour. Bernard growls any time I come close, but I'm worried about her."

"I'm fine," Lolly said from the corner. "Sorry for the trouble, love."

"Oh, it's no trouble at all. I just wanted to make certain you were okay. Bernard wouldn't let me near."

"Good boy, Bernard." Lolly patted the dog's head. "I'm truly fine. I was up late last night, and the episodes happen more often when I'm tired. Did I hear you're headed back to the station, Mercy?"

I wondered if she'd really been asleep when I arrived.

"Yes, ma'am." I wasn't about to share too much about why.

"He didn't go home last night?" She posed it as a question.

"Right. Busy with a case," I said.

Paisley's eyebrows went up as she loaded pastries into the boxes.

"Any news on the murder?" Lolly asked.

"I don't know," I said. "He wasn't really in the mood for sharing, which is why I'm here to grab a bribe. But there is something that I need to talk to you about."

I sat down at her table.

"Anything, dear. You know that."

"Did Lizzie speak to you about the manuscript in the contest?"

She nodded. "But as I said, to keep things fair it's all electronic and done by numbers. We only know the winners when they show up with the number they received in their entry email."

I made a face.

"That isn't what you wanted to hear."

"No, it's not that. Mercy had told me the same. But I wondered if maybe, if that one doesn't win one of the places, there is a way we could do something like an honorable mention. Then when the person came to collect, we would know."

"Hmmm. We've never manipulated things like that with this contest. Well, with any of our contests."

"Right. I completely understand. But it was actually pretty good writing. I don't know how the others rated it, but I gave it a high score. Not because I think the writer may be a murderer. It was good."

"I see."

"I'm not certain what my sister and Caro have scored the entries, but this might help us in Kieran's investigation."

She frowned. "I heard a rumor this morning that he rounded up a bunch of men last night and thought one of them was the killer."

Nothing made it past the detective inspector's gran.

"Uh. That might be a rumor but I'm not certain it's true."

"You were there," she said pointedly.

"Only for a few minutes, and to take him the manuscript. They seemed so tired, I thought I'd bring them back some treats."

"Hmmm. That's kind of you. What did you ask for in return?"

I adored Lolly, but she missed nothing.

"Just trying to follow in my sister's footsteps with a bit of kindness. Nothing has been promised." I smiled sweetly.

"Go on, you. Tell him to check in with his gran. I was worried when he didn't go home. It's why I didn't sleep."

I grinned. Not long ago he'd moved in next door to her. He liked the idea of being able to keep a closer eye on her, but I'm not sure that was what had happened. I had a feeling he might have been regretting that choice, as she constantly spied on him. He adored her though.

"I'll tell him."

She shooed me away.

"I don't feel right charging you if it's for the station. I usually give them things for free. They do so much for all of us."

"Nope. I'll be paying you." I plopped some twenties on the counter. Then I balanced the coffee and two boxes of pastries.

"I know you're busy writing, but I have a once-a-month get-together with some of my girlfriends. I wondered if you and

Lizzie might like to join us. It's at my house on Sunday after-noon. We play board games, drink too much tea and chat. Very informal."

"That's kind of you. Let me check with Lizzie, she runs my schedule when we are in town. And I may have been volun-teered for one-too-many committees for the fête. I'm still not sure how that happened."

She laughed. "That Marianne is good at getting people to do what she wants."

"She definitely is. Like I said, I'll check with Lizzie."

She nodded. "Do you need help with all that?"

"No, I'm fine."

Thankfully, the station was only a block up the hill.

My only problem was balancing everything, so I could open the door at the station. But Sheila was there pushing it open for me.

"How did you know I was out here?"

She pointed to a camera that faced the door. "You popped up on my screen."

"I see. I should find out what kind of cameras you use. We seem to have had a visitor in the backyard last night."

"Oh?" She appeared confused.

"You didn't tell me about that," Kieran said as he came into the lobby.

I handed him the box of coffee. "You've been busy. Lizzie and Mr. Poe scared them off. At least, she thinks it was a human. That's why I didn't call you. That, and I knew you were busy. She thought she heard someone running, but it could have been a squirrel. Mr. Poe is not a fan of anything encroaching on his territory."

"Rightfully so," Kieran said. "Come on, you can tell me the rest. I'm still waiting on the wife. She had to find someone to watch their children."

I left one of the boxes of pastries with Sheila and took the other one back to Kieran's office. The cottage wasn't that big, but it had a small jail attached. The interview rooms were decorated with floral wallpaper, and the rest of the team had desks in the back room.

"Do you want me to take these back to your team?"

He took the box from me and sat it on his desk. "Sheila can share her box. I'm starving." He poured himself a coffee. And he sighed after that first sip.

I did the same thing.

"Why are you grinning?"

I shrugged. "I have the same reaction to that first sip."

He took a napkin, and two of the pastries. "I'll be right back. Unless you want one?"

I shook my head.

He carried the pastries and coffees off to the team.

"Okay, tell me what happened last night?" he asked. "Do you think it had anything to do with the case?"

"How could it? If you're right about Lewis, you were busy rounding him up. Like I said, she only heard Mr. Poe make a strange noise and thought there were footsteps."

"Don't you have security back there?"

"Only a camera by the door. I didn't know about your problem with the apple tree."

He grunted. "If I don't oversee it, it's never done right," he grumbled. "It will be fixed, but we have to wait until the next quarter for budgetary reasons."

"I get the red tape problem. I was curious what kind of cameras you use here. The ones I have I bought on the internet, and then had an installer come out."

"I offered to help you with that," he said. It wasn't a complaint.

"You have other priorities."

He opened up his desk drawer and moved some things around.

"This is the security company we use." He handed me a card.

"Thanks." I put it in my pocket.

His desk phone rang, and he answered.

"Put her in interview one. Offer her a tea or coffee."

He ran a hand through his hair.

"Are you certain this couldn't have waited until tomorrow. It's just that you all seem exhausted."

"I have to catch a killer," he said.

EIGHTEEN

Kieran typed some stuff on his computer, and then he stood. "You can watch from here." After picking up a thick file from his desk, he was out the door.

I sat down at his desk and waited. The wife wrung her hands nervously. But when Kieran walked in, she put her hands under the table.

She doesn't want him to see she is nervous. *Hmmm*.

"Mrs. McGuilly, thank you for coming in."

"Kieran, we've known each other all our lives. What's this about? Do you have my husband? What did he do this time? I'll not be paying his bail if it's for gambling—again. I give him an allowance each week, if he doesn't have the money to pay you, he's on his own."

I sat back in the chair. I didn't blame her. She seemed like a no-nonsense sort.

"Cat, I asked for you to be here about another matter," he said. His voice was calm and matter-of-fact. "Concerning you."

Her eyes went wide, and the surprise was evident. "Me? I don't understand."

He opened the file. Then he pulled out a photo. I couldn't see who was in it.

"I need to ask about your relationship with Jeremy Lynch."

She frowned. "Who? Clara's husband? The man who died?" Confusion was evident by the way she glanced at the picture and then back at him.

"Were you having an affair with the victim?"

"What!" she screeched. "No. Clara is a friend of mine. Who would say such a thing? Does my husband think I'm having an affair? When would I do that? When I'm hanging out the laundry for the third time in a day, or taking care of his twins? Maybe, it's when I'm at the market buying groceries, or cooking for a family of six, plus whatever blokes he brings home with him. Oh, maybe it's at five in the morning when the youngest wakes up. An affair? As if I have the energy."

I laughed. There was no faking that sort of outrage.

"I have a witness that says they saw you flirting in the pub."

She shook her head and rolled her eyes. "When was this? I haven't had a night out in a year. I was there with the kids a few weeks ago. But there was no flirting. Who is this witness? I'd like to knock them upside the head. If it's my husband, you may be investigating another murder soon."

Whoa. She is angry.

"The witness said Jeremy pulled you into an embrace at the bar."

She made a strange face. "What? Oh. Oh. No. It isn't what you think. He thought I was someone else. I forgot about that. Nearly punched him in the gut. He twirled me to him, but when he saw my face, he put his hands in the air. Did your witness tell you that? I like Clara, except for that moment I can't say I've ever even been near her husband. God rest his soul. I heard he's dead."

"What did he say to you that night?"

She rubbed her forehead. "I don't know. I had to wee.

That's all I could think of. Maybe, something like, 'Sorry, love, thought you were my girl.' I shoved away from him and headed to the ladies. Dear Lord, Kieran, if that is why you think I killed a man, you aren't nearly as good at your job as I thought."

Kieran smirked. "So, you and the victim never met at the beach hut his family owns?"

She sat back and crossed her arms. "Now, that's a tale if ever I heard one. Who was watching my children when all this was happening? Do you know how much a sitter is these days? If I'm to pay for one, I'll be spending my time sleeping. Or maybe getting me hair done. It's been an age. I wouldn't be spending it with the likes of that man.

"Though, I have heard tales that he is a philanderer. But it's gossip. I'm not sure if I should be flattered or furious that someone thinks I'd have the time or the inclination." She brushed her dark hair behind her ears.

Something she said, though, clicked in my head. Jeremy had said she looked like his girl. Clara had differently colored hair. Who did Jeremy think she looked like?

It was weird, but I took a picture of her with my phone. Lizzie knew everyone and was discreet. She could maybe help me with that.

The news that Jeremy may have had an affair might have been true. That incident in the bar was definitely a clue that he'd been up to something.

After a few more minutes, Kieran let her go. Well, first he explained they were holding her husband on several charges and that he was waiting for a lawyer.

She huffed. "Eejit. Like he can afford that. Better be a free one, he'll not be getting a cent from me." She headed out.

Kieran came back into the office. "That did not go as planned," he said.

"Who told you about the affair?"

"One of the men we brought in last night."

"Did he say for certain it was her?"

He shrugged. "Said he wasn't sure, but he'd seen them together in the pub. But there is a hundred percent chance the witness was drunk at the time. I knew I shouldn't have believed him."

"What if she only looked like her? She said he made a mistake. From behind, he'd thought she was someone else. But who?"

He grinned. "That's my job."

"I know. And I'll leave you to it. I need to go home and write. Thanks for letting me listen into the conversation. It actually gave me an idea for my book." I held up my hands in surrender. "I will make it different enough that no one will ever know."

He nodded. Then he yawned.

"Try to get some rest," I said. And then I left.

At the bookstore, Caro sat at the front counter reading.

"Is Lizzie here?"

"In the back, taking her break." She motioned toward the back of the store.

"Thanks. Do you like the book? I read it in school, I think." She was reading *White Nights*, a short story by Dostoevsky.

"I hadn't heard of it until Lizzie mentioned it during one of the book clubs. I've never been a huge fan of Dostoevsky, sometimes a bit wordy for me. But I like this so far."

"And it's short."

"There is that. If I'm honest, I prefer your books. I like a murder story or a thriller."

"I do my best to read all genres, but we have that in common." I waved and then went to the back of the store. Lizzie wasn't in the breakroom. She was in the office at the computer with Mr. Poe curled in her lap. She had pencils sticking out all over her head.

"You busy?"

"Balancing the books," she said without turning away.

"Okay. I'll save it until you come home."

She frowned and then spun her chair around. Mr. Poe grumbled, and she put a hand on his head.

"Save what?"

"I don't want to bother you while you're doing math."

"It's not a big deal. What do you need?"

I pulled my phone out of my pocket. "Do you know Cat McGuilly?"

She took it and glanced at the picture. "I do. She likes true crime and buys a lot of children's books. Her kids are well behaved. She likes bringing them here because they love books and it keeps them occupied so she can browse."

I grinned.

"Why?"

"I was curious if she reminds you of anyone else."

"I don't understand. Like one of the characters in your books?"

"No, in real life. Does she remind you of anyone?"

She glanced at the picture again. "Lots of women have dark-brown hair around here. I can't say that she does."

"Okay. No worries."

"Is that it?"

"Yep. Do you need me to take Mr. Poe?"

He groaned like moving might be the worst idea ever.

"We just came back from a walk. He's good. You headed home?"

I nodded.

"Be careful."

"I always am."

She laughed. "If only."

"Oh, I spoke to Lolly about the thing."

"And?"

"She's thinking about it. Hopefully, Kieran will have cleared the case since the winner's announcement isn't until the first day of the fête."

"Okay. And I agree. I think the whole town is on pins and needles wondering if there is a terrible killer about."

"Oh, also, I was at the bakery and Paisley invited us to a girls' afternoon on Sunday. She says they play board games and drink tea. She wants us to go. It's up to you."

She frowned. "I'm in. Wait. Maybe. I need to check to see when some of our committee meetings were rescheduled. I wrote them down at home. Can I ask you a question?"

"Anything."

"Are you going to make friends or to work on your police investigations?"

I shook my head. "Not everything is about the case. I like Paisley and it never hurts to make friends."

Of course, that didn't mean I wouldn't ask about the case if the opportunity arose.

NINETEEN

After writing my required pages for the day, I felt like a superhuman. It had been so long since I'd written that much. For once, I actually followed the synopsis I'd given to my editor. She would be shocked.

I took a hot shower and then wrapped my hair in a towel. My bed appeared enticing. I still hadn't caught up on my sleep. My superhuman abilities faded fast once I was relaxed.

I threw on some sweats and my slippers. Then I headed to my grandfather's library. Sure, it was ours now, but in our minds it would always be his. He'd kept letters in various books and made it a bit of a treasure hunt for us to find them. Through the letters he told us about his wife, our grandmother, and his earlier life.

There were also a few stories about our father. They had lost touch when our dad went into the military. Grandfather thought he might be a spy. Or he had been killed in action and the government was keeping it a secret.

Our grandfather was a big reader. The bookstore had been his. So, we weren't sure how much of what he wrote was truth or fiction. He did like to spin a yarn, and we enjoyed them.

Lolly had filled in some of the blanks, but when it came to our dad, she'd put up her hands. "They never got along. Two hard-headed men. You know how it is," she'd say.

But we didn't. We grew up with a single mom who had given us an incredible life. We'd been lucky that way. When we asked Mom about our father, she'd been so sad, it would be years before we tried again. Then we eventually gave up.

Since arriving in Ireland, we'd sent letters to the government to ask about him but hadn't heard anything back. We were told it could be years before someone would look through the records to help.

Then, there had been a man in the hospital a few months ago. He'd been hit by a car, and he'd mentioned mine and my sister's name. But we'd been out of town. By the time we came back, he'd disappeared. Kieran thought he might be some crazed fan, and we were better for not knowing.

I wasn't so sure. I sometimes wondered if our dad might be the person who stalked us. But then the immediate question was why? It didn't make sense.

I shivered. I tried to put it all from my mind. I couldn't imagine a father doing that to his kids. It was just my active imagination.

I came in here to relax. One of the fun things I liked to do was find our grandfather's favorite books. It was easy, since those novels had been well-read. He also kept several journals with reviews of every book he'd ever read. Or at least, that is what we thought. There were two shelves of his journals. We liked to read his comments and quite often agreed with his summations of the novels.

Not only did he keep my books in his store to sell, but he had three shelves dedicated to them in here. He'd mentioned how proud he was of us both. From all accounts, he was a kind and gentle man. One who knew how to find the right book for a person.

People claimed my sister and I had the same gift. I wasn't so sure about that.

He had a few first edition Tolkiens, which were gorgeous. But he also had well-worn paperback copies of the same books. I loved the story behind the stories. Tolkien had support from his fellow writer friends while he was writing *The Lord of the Rings*. One of his friends was C.S. Lewis.

"Oh, to be at those dinner parties."

I loved my writer friends and missed the ones I'd left behind in New York. I'd promised them we'd video chat soon when I'd been there for my signings.

"Mercy?" Lizzie called out.

I glanced at my phone. She was home early.

"In the library. Is everything okay?"

"I thought about something for the case. I have an idea. I need to let Mr. Poe out, meet me in the kitchen."

I put the book away and shut the door behind me.

"What's going on?" I asked as I came down the hall. "I thought you were working on the accounts."

"I finished an hour ago. How was your writing?"

"It went well today. But I don't want to jinx myself. What are you so excited about?"

"Well, you asking me about Cat got me to thinking. Whoever hurt Mrs. Walsh was probably at the bookstore that night, right?"

"We don't know that for certain. There was a lot of the poison in her system, and her health was failing, so the ME couldn't be sure about when the injection happened."

"But you think it happened at the store, right?"

"Yes. Because no one noticed the mark on her neck. I remembered signing her books and I hadn't seen it then."

"Right. So, it could be someone who was there. I have the list that we gave to Kieran. Then you told me that he was trying to find a woman who looked like Cat."

"I'm not following."

She sighed. "I thought you'd be more into this."

I grinned. "I'm just not following the logic."

"We check the list against their photos. Perhaps one of the women looks like Cat."

"Ohhhh."

She smiled. "Exactly. I feel so helpful."

"You are. But tell me again how we will do this without photos?"

She snorted. "Even in Ireland people are on social media and search engines."

"Brilliant."

"I know. That person may not have killed anyone, but if Jeremy was having an affair, maybe it was with one of them. I mean, it could be one of the men you saw last night, or the woman Jeremy was having an affair with. We just don't know yet. At the very least, maybe we can determine some suspects. I know Kieran is working that angle as well."

I grinned. "Listen to you sounding all detective-like. Let me grab my laptop."

We sat down at the table with her spreadsheet of the guests at the book signing, and my computer. First, we looked at the women. Within a certain age bracket, we found them online. But some of the older women were mentioned in local newspaper articles. I took pictures of the ones who had dark hair, no matter the age, with my phone, and printed them out.

My sister and I worked better with visuals.

We made two rows, one with the dark-haired women. The second row was of people at the book signing who may have had some sort of problem with Eva, Jeremy, or both.

When we'd finished, we stared at the rows. There were far too many in each one.

"How do we start whittling it down?" Lizzie asked.

"I think we look at it from a different angle," I said.

"What do you mean?"

"It's possible that we're looking at someone who crossed paths with both of our victims. A person who needed them dead for some reason."

"That's so extreme," she whispered.

"But true."

"We say this almost every time, but what if the murders aren't connected," she said.

"That's always a possibility. But you know I don't really believe in coincidences." I held up my hands. "I know that you do. The murders are too close together. Both victims had trouble with others. One had a gambling problem and was a womanizer. The other a gossip, who was known for spreading rumors."

It hit me.

"You have that weird look in your eye. What does it mean?"

"A rumor about her womanizing grandson-in-law."

"I don't understand. You think he killed her? But he wasn't there that night, and then who killed him?"

"No. What if the person he had an affair with was threatened or blackmailed by them?"

"This is Shamrock Cove," she said. "It's a small town and that sometimes feels like a soap opera when you find out people's secrets. That said, to murder or blackmail someone feels so extreme."

"To protect face? We've seen people murder for less." I was thinking about one of the former cases we worked on here in the village.

Her shoulders sagged. "You make a good point. How do we find out who it was, though? And are you saying the killer is a woman?"

I shrugged. "Or an angry spouse or lover. You hear more than most in your store. Do you have any ideas?"

"No. I adore Clara. I hate to think of Jeremy cheating on

her. But the lipstick I found on his clothes at their house sort of sealed that deal."

I patted her hand. "I understand that, but we have to think like a killer. What did the murderer have to lose? Reputation? Money? If we can figure out the motive, it might lead us to the perpetrator."

"Do you think Eva was capable of blackmailing someone? Wouldn't saying her grandson-in-law was a cheater harm her family's reputation and hurt Clara? She maybe wasn't the nicest woman, but she loved her granddaughter. She bragged about Clara and the kids."

"But never Jeremy, right?"

"You know how families can be. I feel lucky to have had our mother. She always looked out for us. We made mistakes and she was there for us. I hate that she's gone, but I'm so grateful for the way we grew up."

I smiled. Then I hugged her. "I couldn't agree more."

"Okay, let's focus on what we do know. Jeremy had an affair with a dark-haired woman. Could she be one of these women?"

We had seven photos of women who were of various ages.

"I think we can definitely rule Marianne out," she said. "I can't see her having an affair with someone like Jeremy. I mean, I didn't know him. She's so uptight, my guess is she'd want someone she could control."

I laughed.

"What?"

"Look at you profiling."

She shrugged. "I've known her a while now."

"I hear you, but sometimes we do crazy things for love. We can't count her out quite yet. Are any of these other women on the fête committees?"

"Well, yes. Most of them have been roped in by Marianne for one thing or another. Why?"

"You and I will be going to a lot more meetings in the next few days. I need you to get the schedules."

"Shouldn't you just take all of this to Kieran?"

"He'd laugh. We have no evidence. You know how casual conversations can sometimes be revealing. And we'll ask our little Scooby Gang to help. We're just diving in a bit deeper than we did before. It isn't a big deal."

"Unless we nudge the killer in our direction."

She had a point, and it had happened before.

"We'll be extra careful."

TWENTY

Two days later, there was a big meeting for all the committee members in the back room of the Crown and Clover. As usual, I'd nearly forgotten. Thank goodness for alerts on my phone. I'd actually been speaking to Carrie, my editor, for the last half hour. She wanted to know about the tour, and, of course, where I was with the next book.

For once, I could tell her I was in a good place. At least, as long as these writing spells lasted. I never missed a deadline, but more often than not, I wrote until the last possible moment before my books were due. I didn't like it, but I'd learned to accept it as part of my process. I called it deadline panic. It brought the words to me faster than usual.

After my suggestion that we should attend more of the meetings, my sister had gone to Marianne and suggested one big meeting to make sure everyone knew the bigger plan. Marianne had thought that was a great idea.

Mr. Poe and I met Lizzie outside the bookshop. She locked the door. "Are you closing for the day?"

"It's been slow, and Caro and I are both on committees. It's just easier."

"Do you think maybe you should hire someone else part-time?"

She nudged my shoulder. "That's why I have you. But no. Until the holiday season Caro and I can handle it. Though, a couple of interns from the summer are coming down to run the booth at the fête over the weekend."

"That's nice of them."

"They are like family, now. I was heartbroken when they all went back to university."

I'd been on tour, so I'd missed the goodbyes. But they were a good crew.

"Did you tell our gang what we're doing today?" She reached down and rubbed Mr. Poe on the chin. Everyone had to pay the Mr. Poe toll. If he wasn't greeted properly, he'd pout.

"Each person has a specific target, as do you and I."

"Target sounds so professional. It's making me nervous."

I put my arm through hers. "You know better than that. We're just getting to know people. It's good for your business, right?"

"Argh. You know that it isn't."

"It's all about attitude. You're the friendliest person I know. You just have to be yourself. Leave the detecting stuff to me."

"Okay."

"I mean it. If you talk to someone you think might be suspicious, then give me the hand signal."

"It's so spy-like."

"Think of it as a game. You've got this. I've seen you in your element around people. You're so much better than I am at that sort of thing."

I wore graphic T-shirts that said things like, *I'm all peopled out*. We were twins, but we couldn't be more different. I had the Irish side with my strawberry-blonde hair, and my sister had dark hair from our Italian ancestors on my mom's side. Her parents had been Irish and Italian. They had passed by the time we were born, and our mom had truly been on her own with twins. I didn't know how she did it, but our house had always been filled with love. My sister and I never once questioned if we were loved, and we understood how lucky we were.

When we arrived at the pub, Matt motioned us toward the back room. But then he waved me over.

"I'll meet you in there." I gave Lizzie Mr. Poe's leash.

Then I headed to the bar. "What's up?"

"A little bird told me that you were looking for one of Jeremy's women," he whispered across the bar.

"One of?"

"He was pretty awful in that way. I always felt sorry for poor Clara and her kids. Though it could be he was just a big flirt, but we'd had a few complaints about him being handsy. I kicked him out for a few months. I meant to tell you that the other day. He was only recently allowed back in. That was due to Clara, who likes to eat here with the kids. When she asked why he wasn't welcome, I couldn't tell her the truth."

"Do you think she knew?" She was so kind I'd never considered Clara as a possible killer.

"Doesn't the wife always know something? Even if they don't want to admit it?"

"Maybe, in a town this small. But she didn't seem to when we spoke to her. And I saw her reaction to the deaths. No one is that good of an actress."

"You may have a point."

"So, what were you going to tell me?"

"He had a type. Complete opposite of his wife. But the truth is I remembered something about the night he died. I need to tell Kieran, but maybe you could relay the message."

"Of course, though if I tell him he's still going to want to talk to you. He likes info straight from the witness. What did you see?"

"I was taking out the rubbish that night and I heard him

talking to someone on the other side of the pub. It was a woman, but they were whispering. I couldn't tell what they were saying. When I dumped the bags in the bin, they heard and walked off."

"Could you see who it was?"

"No. She had dark hair though. The outside light from the pub caught them as they walked away."

"Interesting. Were they canoodling?"

"I have no idea what you mean by that."

"Did they act like they were lovers or were they arguing?"

"Ah. Definitely appeared to be arguing."

"Were they headed toward the beach huts down on the shore?"

"Yes, they were going in that direction. But it was dark. Once they were out of the light, I couldn't see much. Do you think that will help narrow down the killer, and do you think it was that woman? Maybe I was the last one to see him alive?" He frowned deeply. "I hadn't thought of that before. I'm mad at myself for forgetting. We were just so busy, it hadn't registered until now."

"I don't know the answers to that, but it might help Kieran with his investigation. I'm going to text him. I need to go into the meeting. But just tell him everything that you told me if he comes by."

"I don't like the idea that we had a killer in the pub."

"We don't know that. Though, did you see him with a woman in here? Maybe, that same dark-haired woman?"

"Like I said, he had a type. But he only flirted a bit, as far as I saw. He didn't seem to mind if they were a bit older or a lot younger."

"Oh?"

"He'd dance with women and maybe whisper a few things. But nothing that would label him as a cheat in public. From what I understand that wasn't exactly the case."

"You mean the rumors of his philandering outside the pub. Who is talking about that?"

He shrugged. "Everyone. Seems everyone is saying his past caught up with him. Maybe an angry husband or a debt being called in."

I had considered both the husband and debt angle and felt the pieces were beginning to fall into place.

"Thanks for the info. Like I said, I'll text Kieran. You've been super helpful."

I was now more determined than ever to find the dark-haired woman.

The meeting was blessedly short. Thanks to Marianne's organization, the head of each committee had exactly two minutes to give their final reports before the big day.

There were snacks, tea, and coffee for after, and everyone stuck around. I watched as my friends and sister made beelines to their assigned targets. It was all I could do not to smile.

"Any news on the cases?" Marianne asked.

"Cases?"

She gave me a tight smile. "Everyone knows you're working with the detective inspector. You've been seen coming and going from the station." Her eyebrows went up. "Unless that is for another reason."

I cleared my throat. "If I were helping the police, I wouldn't be able to share anything."

"So, no word yet if it was murder?"

Her tone made me suspicious. She did have dark hair, and I had suspected her when I'd heard about the past with Clara's grandmother and that her husband had been a diabetic. She was fit and pretty in an angular way. Still, I couldn't see her with Jeremy. My sister was right. She was too uptight.

"I couldn't say. I know you had some words with Eva in the past."

She waved a hand. "It was in the past. She was a dear friend. I'd forgiven her for the meanness. I've said that."

"Did you know her grandson-in-law?"

She laughed and rolled her eyes. "Why would I? He was a rough sort. Not sure what Clara ever saw in him. She deserves someone as kind as she is. Sorry. I shouldn't have laughed. He's dead. I should be respectful. He wasn't a good sort, though. Everyone knew it—except maybe his family. They never seemed to catch on."

"What did Eva think of him?"

"Well, that's another story. She was never a fan. You know why they had to move in with her. It had nothing to do with her health. If she was killed, he would have been at the top of my page when it came to suspects."

"Did you ever witness any altercations between them?"

She shook her head. "I try to stay out of others' business. I keep myself busy with all of my commitments."

"I asked before, do you know of anyone who would really want to hurt Eva? You've had some time to think about it."

"She rubbed people the wrong way, but so do a lot of villagers. I can't see anyone killing her over a bit of gossip."

"I never said she was killed."

She waved a hand. "You didn't have to. You've been asking me questions and why would they take so long to release poor Eva's body if it weren't murder. Why would you be so curious if she hadn't been killed? I'll need to speak to the detective inspector. It won't do to have a killer running around during the fête. Do you think they can keep it out of the press? The publicity could kill our crowds."

Then she turned and walked away.

Hmmm. The woman didn't exactly have her priorities straight. But my sister was right, I didn't see her as a killer.

Brenna waved me over to meet her target. "I wanted to introduce you to Petunia," she said.

"Please call me Tuni," she said. "I'm a big fan of yours."

"Oh? Well, thanks."

"Tuni was telling me that Jeremy hit on her at the founders fête a few months ago," Brenna whispered.

Tuni rolled her eyes. "I complained to Matt, and he threw him out of the pub. It was obvious he was drunk, but he kept trying to get me to dance with him. When he grabbed me, I shoved him away. He tripped and fell down. Then he got mad real fast. Bless Matt for jumping in and showing him the door."

"I'm sorry you had to go through that," I said.

She shrugged her shoulders. "Thank you. People kept telling me he was just drunk, but I don't see that as an excuse. Also, I have a boyfriend, Tom. I was out with my friends having a girls' night out and Jeremy wouldn't leave us alone. Thought he was God's gift or something."

"Drunk people do sometimes think highly of themselves," Brenna said.

"Good for Matt sending him out the door," I said. "Did he give you any trouble after that?"

She shook her head. "Like I said, Matt banned him from the pub for a long time. And I know you'll wonder if it was my Tom who might have hurt him." She held up a hand. "We've all heard the rumors he was murdered. But Tom is in Belfast on a construction site. He won't be back in town for an age."

"Do you know if he had problems with anyone else?"

"I hate to say it, but I'd say most of the single women in this room and some of the married ones. He was not very particular, if you know what I mean."

The more I learned about Jeremy, the less I liked him. Maybe, he'd been good to his family, like they said. But he didn't seem to be a decent human being.

"Have you heard of a husband or boyfriend being angry?"

She shook her head. "I think most of us blew him off. And our Irishmen can be a bit jealous. No use raising a fuss."

Again, the jealous husband or boyfriend made sense, but now we had way too many suspects.

I had to talk to Kieran. Maybe he really did have the killer in jail.

One can only hope.

TWENTY-ONE

I adored our neighbor Rob for many reasons, but his culinary skills might have been the main one. He was quite the chef and as humble as they came. That hadn't been my experience with those in the culinary world. We were so lucky that he loved trying out his new recipes on us. Dinner at his house was something we did quite often, and that connection had helped those who lived closest to us become some of our dearest friends.

The court neighbors were scheduled to meet at his house at six. That's where we planned to discuss what we'd found out after the big committee meeting. He said he had a surprise cuisine for us. I couldn't wait for the food and the information. I'd texted Kieran about what we would be doing and that he was invited.

I had just pulled on my boots, when the doorbell rang. Mr. Poe barked. I thought maybe Lizzie had forgotten her key, but it wasn't his bark for her. When I peeked through the small window in the top of the door, Kieran was there.

"I thought you might meet us for dinner at Rob's."

"I'm going. I want to hear what the others have to say, but I have something to tell you."

"Oh?"

"I'd like to keep this between us."

I nodded. "Follow me to the kitchen. I need to let Mr. Poe out."

We sat down at the kitchen table. "What's happened? Did you find the killer?"

"No. I've had to let Lewis go. Though he was charged for several counts of illegal gambling."

"Did he have an alibi for the murders?"

"He did. Matt gave me the CCTV for the front of the pub. Lewis was there until well after Jeremy was killed."

"Did they by chance figure out who the woman was that Matt heard Jeremy talking to in the back? Maybe you caught them on CCTV?"

"Thanks for that information, by the way." He seldom said anything like that, though he was more amenable about me working on cases. "There weren't any cameras between the back of the pub and the beach huts. We have some pointed toward the beaches and water, but nothing along that path."

"Hmmm."

"The main reason I wanted to talk to you was cause of death for Jeremy."

"The tests came back. Was it insulin?"

"It was."

"That means it is most likely the same killer."

"Agreed. And they are both murders, officially, that is."

"People already suspect murder. You know how this town is. You won't be able to keep it a secret for long."

"I've threatened my team that if they spill they risk losing their jobs. You're the only one, besides the ME, who knows. I'm only telling you because this person has killed two people. I need you to be careful with your—"

"Snooping?"

"Investigation," he finished, but we both knew he meant snooping.

"Let me grab my notebook. I wrote some things down earlier that I couldn't remember if I told you."

I grabbed the leather notebook from my office. It was the same one I kept my story ideas in as I wrote. Things came to me out of the blue, so it was always with me.

"Okay, there's something here I hadn't thought about before and we can ask the others tonight."

"What's that?"

"The lipstick Lizzie found on Jeremy's shirt. She took a picture. Unfortunately, the shirt was washed so that DNA is probably gone. But we could perhaps match the color with the woman."

He shrugged. "You think a woman overpowered a man the size of Jeremy?"

"If he was drunk, and it sounds like he was, yes. He may not have even felt the needle. The bruise was on the back of his neck. She could have pretended to hug him. Or he could have passed out drunk and then the drug was administered."

"He would have been dead weight then. How would a woman be able to shove him under the hut like that?"

"I'd have to do an experiment, but the sand is very soft there. And his feet were sticking out. There were short drag marks. Oh."

"What?"

"It had rained. Remember? Next to the steps leading into the hut, it appeared like the tide had come up. But what if someone washed or brushed away their footprints? They could have used a bucket, and a bit of ocean water, and we would have assumed it was the rain. Also, we can't assume it was one killer. I mean, my gut says it is one, but it could have been two killers, right? How about DNA on the body?"

"You make a good point. It was a mess at the crime scene.

We're still waiting on DNA. It always takes longer. But both bodies will be released to the funeral home tomorrow. From what I understand, there will be a combined wake and funeral. Gran helped Clara make the arrangements. Gran said she was a mess. Those are Gran's words."

I took a deep breath. "My sister and I can relate. Making all those decisions when you're grieving is tough. Bless your gran for looking after her. Lolly really is good when it comes to the details."

My phone buzzed. "It's time to head over to Rob's. You coming?"

"I need to go home and change, I'll meet you there. And remember, keep the news I gave you close."

"It won't be easy, they already know we suspect murder. But they won't hear it from me," I promised.

After he left, I let Mr. Poe in. He waited patiently while I dried him off. There was no need for a leash since we were only going next door, and he was extremely well behaved.

A few minutes later, we were at Rob's. Lizzie had gone over earlier to help him set the table. He loved making food a big spectacle and we loved him for it. My sister answered the door.

Before saying anything to me, she reached down and gave Mr. Poe an ear scratch.

"It smells so good in here," I said.

"Right? My stomach has been grumbling for the last half hour."

"Who is that?" Rob asked from the back of the house. His and Scott's place reminded me of a fancy men's hunting lodge, but in a way that might make the pages of *Architectural Digest*. Everything was perfectly designed.

"It's me," I said as we headed toward the back of the house. "Is there anything I can do to help?"

"We're set. I'm just finishing up."

The doorbell rang. "I'll get it," Lizzie said.

I went into Rob's proper chef's kitchen, with stainless steel everything. "Can I carry anything to the table? Is that butter chicken I smell?"

He laughed. "I'm doing a mixture of Indian and Nepalese tonight. The favorite will become a part of the menu for the fête. I'm doing an around-the-world spectacular, and I'll have a few Irish faves. But the pub has so much of that covered. Though, I'm being picky on exactly what I want to serve."

"You are amazing, and so is your food. That said, I'm always grateful that you love trying things out on your friends."

"I've been feeling so lonely without my Scott. I'm happy to have the company."

The doorbell rang again.

He shoved a platter at me. "Take this and put it on the table. Wait until you see how your sister decorated. She is a woman after my own heart. There is a spot that fits the platter in the middle of the table."

A crowd had gathered in the dining room. Kieran was there and took the platter from me. As if he knew exactly what to do, he put it in the middle of the table. Brenna and Lolly had already sat down. My sister's tablescape looked like a colorful market in India, with a brightly colored tablecloth and mix-and-match dishes in a rainbow of shades.

Lizzie pushed past me. "I'll help him bring in the rest."

They returned with two platters each of food.

"Now, all of these are hand-held so people can walk around the fête," he said. "I want your honest opinion about each one. If it's too spicy, or anything that might not be popular for the masses."

We settled down to eat, and everyone was quiet as we tried each dish. True to form, it was all fabulous.

"When do we get to the part where we tell you who killed our poor victims?" Brenna asked.

Kieran coughed and brought his napkin to his mouth. Lolly

patted him on the back. It was all I could do not to giggle. I almost lost it when I saw my sister hide a smile with her hand.

"Are you okay, Kieran?" Rob asked. He wore a smile as well.

"Sorry," Brenna said. "I don't ever get to be a part of the Scooby Gang. I'm so curious about what everyone found out at the pub."

"Why don't we start with you, if that's all right with, Kieran." I pointed to him.

He nodded.

"Other than Tuni, who you talked to as well, I spoke with Sharon Applegate," she said. "Actually, she was nice and she's fairly new to town. She's also into photography so we talked a lot about that."

"Did she by chance know Jeremy or Mrs. Walsh?" I asked, trying to stay on topic.

"She'd heard about it in the news. She thought it was all quite scary and wondered if that sort of thing happened often. I told her, no. She didn't seem to know anything about either of them though. I was disappointed. I wanted to break the case."

"That's my job," Kieran said it under his breath, and I couldn't help but smile.

"I had a good chat with Laura Green," Rob said. "She and Jeremy actually dated in high school. She had nothing nice to say about him. It made me feel even sorrier for poor Clara. As far as Laura is concerned, Jeremy never changed. He was always handsy and flirted with every woman he met. Her words."

"Did she seem like she might want to kill him?" Brenna asked.

Rob shook his head. "No. But you never know. She could have been lying. But she did seem to worry about Clara. She was teary-eyed when she asked if I knew how Clara was doing."

"Anything to do with Eva Walsh?"

"She knew of her," Rob said. "Most everyone did. She was well known as one of the original..." His eyes went wide.

Lolly cocked her head. "One of the what?" she asked curiously.

Rob stared down at his plate.

"Uh, so, Lizzie, how about you?"

Lolly held up a hand. "Wait. I want to know what Rob was going to say. The original what?"

"Dragon ladies," Kieran said. "I'd say it's a compliment."

Lolly stared at her grandson and then hooted with laughter. "Do they really call us that?"

"Yes," Kieran answered honestly. "For as long as I can remember."

"I'm surprised I haven't heard it before. I love it. We should change the name of the book club to The Old Dragon Ladies."

I loved Lolly's sense of humor.

"Well, this dragon spoke to Rachelle, who works for Paisley in the bakery kitchen. She did used to sometimes meet up with that scoundrel, Jeremy. But not for more than a year."

"I can't believe she shared that with you," Lizzie said. "I'd be so embarrassed."

"Oh, she was more than happy to trash his name. Said more than once he promised to leave his wife, and she believed him. She finally gave up when she met Clara for the first time. She said, 'She was such a kind woman, I just couldn't do that to her. But he had lots more after me. He was always after some girl at the pub.'"

"Interesting," Kieran said. For the first time, he took his notebook out of the pocket of his jacket, then took it off and hung it on his chair.

"How about you, Lizzie?" Kieran asked.

My sister ducked her head.

"Uh. Well. You all know Theresa who sometimes works at the pub on the weekends?"

"Yes," we said collectively. Theresa was in her forties, had a long black ponytail that bounced when she walked. She always had a friendly and playful demeanor.

"So, the night that Eva died, it couldn't have been Jeremy who killed her."

Kieran dropped his fork, and it clattered against the plate. "Why is that?"

"She and Jeremy were in his truck that night. And they were, um, very busy." Lizzie's cheeks turned bright pink. "She said he'd bought her shots after her shift, and she wasn't in her right mind. She was embarrassed but thought we should know in case he was a suspect."

"I see." Kieran wrote in his notebook again. "Did she seem jealous of the wife in any way?"

Lizzie shook her head. "No. In fact, in a weird way, she seemed to feel sorry for Clara. She told me how embarrassed she was when she sobered up. But he also told her he'd planned to leave his wife. That's weird, right? Do you think he really was planning on leaving?"

If Clara found out, could she have killed him?

Kieran glanced at me as if he had had the same thought. The wife was usually the most likely suspect, but then it was more than obvious Clara loved her grandmother.

I had so many questions.

TWENTY-TWO

The next night, those on the court had decided to go as a group to pay our respects to the family. Clara and her children held a vigil for her mother and husband in their front room, which was crowded with friends and family. Her children sat around their mother, heads down as Pastor Mark said a prayer. They were all so sad, and my heart hurt for them.

Poor Clara looked as if she was barely hanging on. That was not the appearance of a woman who had revenge on her mind. I'd seen that same look on my sister when our mom, Lizzie's fiancé, and his daughter died. I wasn't sure I'd ever be able to pull her back to the living.

More now than ever, I understand how important our move to Ireland had been for the both of us.

We'd promised Kieran that we wouldn't investigate while we were here. Though, I wondered if I could perhaps sneak into the master bedroom. I wanted to check the pockets of Jeremy's pants and jackets. Men were always leaving bits of paper in their clothes. My sister was very against the idea, but she hadn't thought to go through the things in the closet. She'd only been concerned with what was in the laundry hamper.

After the prayer, we were invited to eat and visit. First, we paid our respects. My sister knew a majority of the family members and made introductions. "They are a family of readers," she kept saying. Eventually, we made our way to Clara.

"I know they're only words, but please know our hearts hurt for you," Lizzie said to Clara and the children. "If there is anything we can do, just ask. We are here for you."

"That's kind of you," Clara said. "It's been..." She brought a tissue to her nose.

"Will you be using our family members deaths for one of your books?" the oldest daughter, Niamh, asked.

"No," I said. "I don't use, um, true crime for my books. And you're Niamh. What are you studying at university?"

"Maths and critical thinking, but I love reading. Like your sister said, we all do. My gran always talked about your books. She said you had to be Irish because you told a good story."

I smiled. "That's kind of you to share that memory." I didn't mean to sound so formal, but she caught me off guard.

"Are you still helping the police?" the oldest son, Kingston, spoke up this time. "Mum says you help out and that if we had questions, we should ask you and not the detective inspector."

"Uh."

"I didn't mean at the family vigil," Clara said softly. "Now is not the time, Kingston."

The boy nodded. "I understand, Ma, but no one will tell us anything. Gran was—unhealthy. So why are they investigating? And Da drank too much. Probably fell and hurt his head. He was always tripping over his own feet."

"Kingston," his mother chastised. "Please. This is no time to speak ill of our family." Clara shook her head. "I'm sorry. They are just curious. Everything has happened so fast. It's too much to deal with all at once." She sobbed a little.

Her son reached his arms around her. "Sorry, Ma. I didn't mean to make a fuss."

The kindness in the young man's voice was my undoing. I had to turn away.

"We'll move along," Lizzie said. "Again, let us know if you need anything."

We moved back toward the small dining room where the food was.

"Wow, that was tough," I said.

"Dredges up our past, doesn't it?"

I nodded. "Definitely hits close to home. Though, in a weird way, we were lucky that we knew exactly how they died right away. I know how awful that sounds, but the unknowing has to be so hard on the family."

"Agreed. When are you heading upstairs?" she whispered.

"Soon. I need you to stand guard in case anyone tries to come up."

"Except for the one in Eva's room, the only bathroom is up there, but I'll try. Just keep your phone handy."

"There are only a few stairs. By the time you texted me, it would be too late. I promise to be quick."

I patted her shoulder. She'd come a long way since we first started investigating. Back then, she'd complain about the stress of possibly being caught. From her grin, I could tell she was excited.

"Stop smiling. It's a vigil. People will wonder if you're up to something."

She cleared her throat. "I always get so nervous. That said, I really want you to find out who the killer is. It's nearly time for the fête, and Marianne says the publicity is terrible for the town. Oh. My. Goodness. Listen to me. I sound like her. You know I'm not like that."

"I do. It's scary to think someone might be running around killing people."

"I agree, and shhhh. She just came in the door."

My sister's eyes were huge. "Do you think she heard me?"

"She looked this way, but I think she was busy surveying the room. She made a beeline for Clara. Besides, I thought you said she was nice."

"She is, but she likes things a certain way and she's all about appearances," Lizzie said. "You're the one who reminded me that we've run into that sort of thing before."

"True. Do you have any reason to suspect her of... you know?"

She snorted. "No. I told you before, she wouldn't hurt a fly. But reputation is important to her. She's in charge of everything for the fête. It's the first time Lolly has given up the reins, and I think Marianne wants to prove herself. Well, I don't think it, I know it. She certainly wouldn't risk killing anyone. That might disturb the image of the fête."

She made a good point.

"Okay, I'm going to slip upstairs quickly. I won't be more than five minutes. One quick look, and I'll be back down."

She blew out a breath. "Okay, let's do this."

After a quick glance around, I found everyone in conversation and none of them paying attention to me.

I slipped up the stairs. It took a couple of doors, but I found the master suite. I should have asked my sister what door it was. I didn't know exactly what I hoped to find, but Lizzie had said she didn't check the clothes in the wardrobe, and perhaps Kieran and his folks had missed something. I doubted it, but I had to check for myself.

The room was cozy with a double bed, which had a quilt spread across it. There was one dresser and a wardrobe. I went straight for his clothes in the wardrobe and the door squeaked when I opened it.

I might have given a slight prayer that no one heard that noise. I waited a few seconds, but nothing happened. There was a slight hint of some kind of men's cologne with musk and maybe sandalwood. I couldn't quite place it. The wardrobe was, however, very organized.

I checked the coats and jackets first. I took any receipts or papers and stuffed them in the pocket of my cardigan. I could sort through them later. And if I did find evidence—well, I'd cross that bridge later with Kieran.

Then I went through the pockets of the jeans and work pants. I found a few more pieces of paper. I was surprised Kieran's team hadn't taken all of these in for evidence. It was possible the papers didn't amount to anything, and this was a huge waste of time.

I was about to check the dresser when a stair creaked.

"Are you certain I can't get it for her?" Lizzie said loudly. "You should stay with your mother. She needs you by her side. I can get the cardigan for you."

I jumped toward the wall side of the bed. It was a tight squeeze between the bed and the wall, but I fit. I lay sideways with my face toward the wall.

"Thank you, but I know right where it is," Niamh said. The door opened and I held my breath.

There were footsteps, and then the squeak of the wardrobe door.

She sniffed. "Oh, Da. I can smell you in here. You weren't perfect but it breaks my heart we won't hear another of your bad jokes." She rummaged a bit. "There it is," she said softly.

There were footsteps, but the door didn't close. I couldn't tell if she was still in the room. Then the bed creaked, as if she'd sat down.

Oh. No. Where was Lizzie?

She sobbed, and my heart cracked a bit more. While I hadn't known our father, my mom's death was the most traumatic thing I'd ever gone through. She'd been my cheerleader throughout my life, and I missed that never-ending support and love.

Then Lizzie's fiancé and his daughter were killed in an accident. I hadn't known them that well, but Lizzie's broken heart nearly did us both in at the time. That was why we'd wanted a fresh start in Ireland.

Niamh sobbed a bit more.

"Oh, hon. Let me get you some tissues," Lizzie said. "I was trying not to bother you, but can I hug you? I'm from Texas. We're huggers." My sister's calm and kind voice nearly had me crying.

"I'm okay," the young girl shuddered.

"You're not and won't be for a long time," Lizzie said. "But I've been where you are. Time really does help. But it sucks big time until then."

That made the girl laugh. "Thank you."

"No problem. Why don't I take this down to your mom? You go freshen yourself up in the bathroom."

"Thanks again. I'll be down in a minute."

When she had left, I popped up.

My sister covered her mouth and made a grunting noise. "You scared me to death. Get downstairs."

I dusted myself off and headed down, she followed not long after.

My pockets were full of papers, but going through them would have to wait.

At the end of the stairs, Kieran stood there gazing up at me.

Great.

"Do I want to know?" he asked as I passed him.

"I have no idea what you're talking about."

He followed me into the dining room where we each took a plate and filled it.

"My team have been over this house already. The warrants came in earlier. What were you doing?" The words were whispered.

"Double-checking something. I promise to tell you when there aren't so many ears around."

He nodded knowingly.

"Any news from the ME?"

"Yes. You found him just three hours after he died. And he was poisoned, but we knew that already."

"Do you have any suspects, other than his gambling buddies?" As soon as I asked the question, I regretted it. It had gone quiet all around us. Crud. "Is this Irish soda bread," I said a little too loud as I pointed to something on the dining-room table. "It's so good, but I always get the breads here confused."

I sounded like I'd lost it, but it wouldn't do for prying ears or eyes to understand what we'd been talking about.

Then I quickly walked away to the other room.

Marianne was seated next to Clara and held her hands.

Lizzie put the sweater around Clara's shoulders.

But it was the look Clara gave Marianne that made me wonder. I couldn't read her face, but it seemed like she might be angry.

Why?

TWENTY-THREE

Later that evening I rode home with Kieran, while Rob, Lizzie, Lolly and Brenna took our car. It was chilly and I appreciated that Kieran was quick to turn on the heater.

"Thanks," I said.

"Now, tell me what you were doing upstairs."

"Well, that didn't take long."

He grunted.

"I went through some of Jeremy's clothes in the wardrobe. I didn't know then that your team had already been there. I found some receipts and scraps of paper in his pants and jackets. I thought that I might find something that would give us a clue."

"And that wouldn't be admissible as you snuck in and retrieved it."

I cleared my throat. "I've been thinking about that. You made me an official consultant."

"Yes, but chain of evidence is a real thing."

I sighed. "Right. Well, let's take a look. Worst-case scenario, I can sneak the papers back into his clothes."

"Mercy."

I held up my hands in surrender. I did that a lot with him. "I know. I know. But we seem to be short on suspects. I thought it was worth a look."

"Fine. But we're stopping at the station and logging it all into evidence. For the record, we'll say I found it. My team should have bagged everything."

"Okay by me. Let me text my sister."

I explained where I was going. And she sent back heart emojis. It was all I could do not to laugh.

At the station, I waved at Greg, who held down the fort at the front desk.

"Follow me," Kieran said.

We ended up in his office. He motioned for me to sit down, and then he pulled some evidence bags out of a drawer. Then he sat across the desk from me. "Let's see it."

I pulled all the scraps out of my pocket. It was more than I thought.

The first one was a petrol receipt, but it wasn't for the gas station here in town. I pointed to the name. "Do you know where this is?"

He frowned. "It's three towns over, and on the way to Dublin."

"But there is a coffee and a tea, and some snacks. That was this past Saturday night. Perhaps it's a reach to say it was a date, but someone was with him. You need to ask Clara what he was doing."

He frowned.

"What is it?"

"Well, we know the next night he'd gone to the pub with his family, then met a woman out the back. This receipt is from the night before. Why wouldn't he be mourning with Clara?"

"We've established he wasn't the greatest person," I said. "I know that's mean, but we have proof. He should have stayed with his family the night he died. If he had, he might still be alive. If he wasn't with his family the night before, maybe he was with the person we've been looking for."

"That is a reach."

"I'm just trying to give you possibilities. Right now, they don't have to make sense. We just need to explore... why are you looking at me like that?"

He smirked. "I've been a copper for a really long time."

I sat back. "I know. I don't mean it as an insult. This is my process as a writer. Disparate things sort of come together in the end to finish the puzzle. It's never a clear path and every piece of information is key for putting together the whole picture."

"Now you're sounding like the detective in your books."

I laughed. "Well, she and I do share a brain."

That made him smile. "There is that, as you like to say. But these receipts made me think of something."

"What's that?"

"There's a small hotel that rents by the hour just outside of that town. Could be that is where he took..."

"His woman, or women?"

"Yes."

"When can we go check it out?"

"In the morning, after ten. I have an interview to do."

"Oh? Who with?"

"Another of Jeremy's friends. I thought he might be at the vigil, but he wasn't. I had Sheila schedule a meet tomorrow."

"Could he be the killer?"

"Doubtful. But he may have known who Jeremy was seeing. There's CCTV of them chatting together several times at the pub, and then outside their store."

"Can I sit in and watch?"

"Don't you have books to write? Besides, it will be brief. I'm only looking for names."

"You're right, I do. So, I'll meet you here at ten?"

"Yes."

. . .

The next morning, I may have been a bit early. I wanted to see who Kieran had been talking to. I'd brought some goodies from the bakery and Sheila had headed back to give them to the team.

"Detective Inspector, our Mercy has brought treats."

He ushered the tall, blond man out the door. He didn't look like anyone I'd seen in town. Though, unlike my sister, I didn't know everyone. He was clean-cut and wore a suit. He didn't look the type to hang out with the dead man.

When the door shut, I asked, "Does he live here?"

"No. Next town over," Kieran said. "But he plays in their poker game a few times a month. Are you ready to go?"

"I brought you a cortado, and these." I held up a bag of chocolate croissants.

He peeked inside and grinned.

"Give me a minute, I'll be back."

He met Sheila in the hall and whispered something. She nodded, and then said, "On it." At least, from my lip-reading course, I thought that was what she said. I wondered what assignment he'd given her.

I followed him out the door, which he held for me.

"I'm grateful you're letting me come along," I said as I climbed into his SUV. "It's good police experience for my writing."

He laughed.

"What? It's true."

"Mercy, we agreed to always be honest with each other."

"Well, it's true. I am grateful to be included."

"Only because you know of the hotel now, and I didn't want you to go there on your own with one of your schemes."

"I feel like that was a big insult, but you're probably right. Is it that bad of a place?"

"No. You'll see."

"But it rents by the hour, that means..."

"We don't have a problem with prostitution if that's where you're going," he said. "It's a place for hikers and tourists, not what you're thinking. A place for people to shower and rest up a few hours before or after they've explored the heather and moorlands."

"Oh." I was so confused.

Kieran gave a wry smile as he drove out of Shamrock Cove.

"Did the guy you just talked to give you any leads?"

He shook his head. "Like the others, he saw Jeremy with a dark-haired woman, but he couldn't identify her. They always met outside of town. That's all he knew, and I believe him. He had no reason to lie. We already knew about the gambling."

"Interesting. Any more from the ME?"

"I told you about time of death. Oh, I forgot. The results for Eva Walsh came in as well. They estimate she received the insulin about an hour before she died. Not only was it injected, but it was also in the stomach contents, which means someone dosed her food."

"You don't think it's anyone in the family, do you?"

He scoffed. "Why would you ask that?"

"I heard the oldest daughter saying her dad wasn't the best. They loved him, but it sounds like they knew he was up to no good."

"Was that when you were hiding upstairs?"

"Perhaps."

"No, we aren't looking at the family. Mainly because of opportunity. Eva was at that book signing an hour and a half before it started. She helped put out flyers for the book clubs. She and some of the other book club members had brought food to share.

"Jeremy had dropped her off early. That's what Clara told us, and Lizzie and Lolly corroborated the story. Then he went to the pub. Clara was only at the book club to hear you speak. Then she left. Sheila's pulling in some of his friends to solidify our timeline to see how long he was at the pub."

"Yikes."

"What's wrong?"

"Just the idea that someone used my book signing to commit murder. It's awful. Poor Lizzie has been hoping the crime actually happened somewhere else. She'll be crushed. She's already worried that people think the place is haunted because of the last murder that happened there."

"But none of it is your fault."

"You and I know that. But she worries the store will get a reputation. I tried to convince her that it would only draw more people in who are curious."

"You're probably right about that."

We laughed.

"We can try to keep the details out of the media. Maybe that will help."

"Thanks. I'm more worried about catching the killer before the fête. Can you imagine having all those people in town while we chase him or her down?"

He shook his head. "It does no good to remind you that this investigation is my job."

"Yep. But a murder happened in our store."

"From what Lolly said, Marianne is more worried no one will show up to the fête because of the murders. Except that I pointed out we haven't gone public with the fact that they were murders."

"Before you ask, I swear no one in my group will say a word. We all have as much invested in the fête as everyone else. And we don't need people acting, well, hysterical, which they will if they find out the truth.

"Also, poor Clara's family doesn't need all that attention. It's bad enough they've lost two people they love. Even if Jeremy was a cheater, and she has to know he was, she doesn't deserve it shoved in her face."

"What do you mean, she has to know he was?"

"Uh. The lipstick on the collars of his shirts. As far as we know, Clara doesn't wear makeup. Lizzie's never seen her in any. She's one of those natural Irish beauties and doesn't need it."

"Oh, right. Lizzie washed the DNA away. I remember now. When you two were helping to clean the house."

"She didn't know better," I said. "She was just being helpful."

"If we had that collar, they may have been able to pull DNA."

"Right. But only if it was in the system. We're talking about Shamrock Cove. How many residents do you think have their DNA in the system?"

"Fair point."

It wasn't long before we pulled up in front of a chateau-like building. It was called the Arms Inn.

"Is this it?"

"It is." He grabbed a file folder from the back seat, and I wondered what was in it.

"It's nice. More Swiss hunting lodge and a lot less seedy motel than I was expecting." We'd passed through a town that was smaller than Shamrock Cove. Most of the buildings had been the old-stone historical type. This appeared to be something new-ish, perhaps built in the last fifty years or so. In Ireland, that was considered modern. Again, one of the many reasons I loved living here. There was so much history.

"It's the detective inspector in for a visit," a big burly man said from behind the front desk, which was intricately carved wood with a brass trim. This really wasn't what I'd been expecting when he said people rented by the hour sometime. "Oh, and he's brought a young lassie with him. Please, introduce me to your beauty." He had a Scottish brogue, but it was the dramatic way he said it all that made me smile.

Kieran shook his head. "Mercy this is Wallace. He and his wife own this establishment. They took over from her parents about ten years ago."

"We did. We run a fine establishment, no matter what this one says." His tone was jovial as he pointed at Kieran.

"It's fine until an angry husband or wife shows up, and we're called in to stop near-murders."

The man held his hands up in a stop motion. "We only provide a wee place for our clients to lay their heads. It isn't up to us to judge if they need a wee bit of company."

I might have snorted at that.

"That's why we're here," Kieran said.

The smile left the other man's face. "We haven't called for assistance."

"I need to know if you have seen this man." Kieran held up his phone.

Wallace squinted at the picture and then his eyebrows went up. "What kind of proprietor would I be if I grassed on our clients?"

"One who wants to help us solve a possible murder," Kieran said.

Wallace took a step back. "He wasn't murdered here," he said.

"Never said he was. I need to know if he was here with a woman, and if you can describe her."

"Oh. No. Word gets around that I'm talking to you and business ends. You know most of our guests are tourists, but we are discreet. He wasn't killed here so it's none of our business."

"I could come by for more regular stops and maybe loiter in

your lobby, or have one of the patrols sit in the parking lot. How would that be for business?"

"Detective Inspector, are you blackmailing me?" The man gasped and put his hand on his chest.

"Some information is all we need, and no one will know you gave it."

The man grunted. "Yes, he comes at least once a week. He was here last Saturday but I can't tell you what the woman looked like. It's always someone different. The last one dressed like some Hollywood type with dark glasses and a coat. And she wore a hat, though she had dark hair underneath.

"What I can tell you is that it wasn't the same woman every time. The rest of them didn't bother hiding their face. He liked them all ages. They usually had dark hair and very red lipstick."

"Would you by chance have a security feed that shows them?" I asked.

"Erases every forty-eight hours. We only have the cameras for insurance purposes. That way if we're robbed, they can catch the thieves."

"Has he been here since Saturday?"

Wallace shook his head. "Like I said, last Saturday he came in and he always paid with cash. Only for a few hours, if you know what I mean."

I did. But we were no closer to finding out who our dark-haired woman was.

"What about the cameras that face the parking lot?" I asked. "I noticed when we were coming inside that you have two pointed that way."

"For car thieves. We had a bit of trouble a while back. Turned out to be some kids messing about. But let me look. Usually, I wipe those once a week just in case something comes up missing in a car."

Kieran and I glanced at one another. Then we went around the desk to the security monitor.

"Saturday, let's see." Wallace hit some arrows. "I can't remember what time he was here."

"It had to be earlier in the evening," I said. "Kieran's been following his movements that night. Maybe, around seven."

The two men glanced at me.

I shrugged. "What? I pay attention."

He moved the arrows slowly.

"There." I pointed to the screen. It was the old farm truck Jeremy used. When he got out, there wasn't a woman in his truck. But he waited by the passenger side, then a woman came into view. No idea where she'd come from, as the camera only showed what was closest to the door.

"She must have parked on the other side of the lot. Do you have cameras there?"

"We do not," Wallace said. "Like I said, we only have the cameras that the insurance demands."

She was covered from head to toe, and it was too dark to see the kind of shoes she wore. There were shadows everywhere.

Jeremy nodded to her, but didn't touch her. That seemed strange, if they were having an affair. If anything, they seemed wary of one another. He gave her quite a look, as if he wasn't at all happy to be in her company.

Interesting.

"And you don't have anything with a clearer picture?" Kieran asked.

"Sorry, Kieran. I can make you a copy of this. Maybe, like on the telly, you have someone who can clean it up for you."

I wanted to say that while forensics had come a long way in the last one hundred years, television often made things appear much easier than they were.

"I'll take it," Kieran said. "At the very least, it helps with our timeline."

"No problem."

"I know this is an odd question, but did he usually ask for the same room?" I asked.

Wallace frowned. "I can't remember, but we can look. I'll pull up his account."

He turned to the computer and pulled up the account by name. "Hmm." He grumbled under his breath.

"What is it?" Kieran asked.

He sighed. "He did. It's our, um, bridal suite. One of those old-fashioned heart-shaped beds. I think it's corny, but it's popular around here."

"I'll need copies of his account."

"I'll print it off. Do you think any of this will help? I give you a hard time, but you have a job to do. And you've always been there for us."

Kieran smiled and patted Wallace on the back. "This helps."

"Kieran— Oh, are you Mercy McCarthy?" a woman said from across the room. She tossed her groceries on one of the round leather benches and half-ran to the desk. "It has to be you. What's going on?"

"If you slowed down and let a person answer, luv, they might explain."

"Hi," I said.

"It is you, right? The author? I've read every single one of your Doctor Drove mysteries. Will they ever make them into a television series? Though it could never be as good as the books. Speaking of which, will you sign them for me? Please. I can't believe you're here."

"I don't think I've ever seen my wife this excited," Wallace said. "Aubrey, luv, slow down a minute."

"If Kieran doesn't mind waiting, I'd be happy to sign your books."

Kieran shrugged. "I need to make a call. I'll wait for you outside."

"Come with me." Aubrey hooked her arm in mine, and yanked me along with her.

It was all I could do not to laugh.

"Our apartment is here on the first floor. I can't believe you're here in person. I wanted to come to your book signing but we had a convention of engineers that day. It was all hands on deck. Isn't that what you Americans say?"

She was Irish. "I'm curious how you met your husband? He's Scottish, right?"

"He is. We met at university. Isn't that funny. I was wondering why you are with Kieran. Are you two dating?"

I had no idea how to answer that. "I help him with cases sometimes."

"Oh, the glamorous life of the author. I always imagine you sitting by the fire while you eat chocolates and come up with amazing stories."

I laughed. "Usually, it's the cookies my sister makes and lots of coffee. But mostly my life is boring. I sit at the computer all day."

"Oh, that isn't true. You just came off a worldwide tour. I read about you online."

"I hope the stories were nice."

"Mostly fans like me talking about how lovely you are."

My cheeks heated. "That's sweet."

"Now, I have them all. And I realize that might be a bit much but I would love it if you could sign them all."

"I'm happy to," I said. I loved a fanatical fan. They were the best. Though, more often than not, they remembered far more about each novel than I did.

"Do you want them signed to you, Aubrey?"

She put her hands on her face. "Would you? That would be wonderful. I treasure my books like works of art. They are that to me."

"I'm happy to." I reached into my bag and was grateful to

find I hadn't emptied it out, which meant it had all of my book-signing essentials. Bookmarks, stickers, and my favorite pen.

"I hate being nosy, but why are you here? I mean, I'm grateful but curious. Did something happen while I was at the shops?"

"No. Like I said, I'm helping Kieran with a case. Turns out a man who was murdered may have stayed here the night before he died."

I glanced up to see her eyes go wide. "Not here. I mean, he died in Shamrock Cove. Kieran's trying to piece together a timeline."

"Who was it? Maybe I'll remember," she said. "I work the desk most days and some nights."

"Jeremy Lynch," I said quietly.

"Oh. He was here. Came in with a different woman this time. Though he likes them with dark hair."

"Did you see her face? Could you recognize her?"

"She wore dark glasses and a coat with a scarf. He did have a type though. Dark hair and red lipstick. That's a strange thing to notice, right? I figured he bought the shade for them because they were all the same. Except for her. Hers was more wine colored. Not the usual orange red."

That was strange.

"Does that help you?"

"It could," I said. It took me nearly a half hour to sign the books. She offered me tea, but I declined. Poor Kieran probably hadn't planned on waiting so long.

"You are the best," she said as she walked me to the front door of the hotel. "I will make the next book signing, I promise. Any idea when the next book will come out?"

"Next one is set for April next year."

"I can't wait. Thank you again."

"Oh, one more thing. Do you know this gentleman?" I showed her a picture on my phone that I'd copied off a website.

"Mr. McCormick?" She grinned.

"What?"

"He does come for a weekend sometimes. He meets with an elderly woman, and they love to go antiquing together. They stay in the same room with twin beds. I don't think it's—well, you know. More like friends meeting up for some fun."

"It wasn't this woman, right?" I showed her a picture of Eva.

"No. Isn't she the one who died? I saw it in the paper."

"She is. I was just curious."

"I wish I could be more help, but I've never seen her."

I waved and headed out to the SUV. Kieran was on the phone. He hung up as I climbed into the car.

"Everything okay?"

I nodded. "She had more books than I was expecting. But I have some interesting news to share."

TWENTY-FOUR

On the way home, we chatted for a bit, and then I asked Kieran if Wallace had been any more forthcoming when I'd left with his spouse.

"He did mention that the visits lasted longer than they had last Saturday."

"Yuck," I said.

He laughed. "You asked. How about you? Any news from Aubrey? If there is tea to spill, she'd be the one."

"I think that is a sexist thing to say. Just because she's a woman she would gossip."

"No, usually if I have an inquiry, I go to her first. Unlike Wallace, she has a keen eye for details. She remembers things that he never even noticed."

"Nice save." I gave him the eye, but he was focused on the road and didn't see it.

"It's the truth. So, what did she say?"

"She remembered that the woman Saturday night wore a different shade of red lipstick. She said it was more wine colored."

"And?"

"Well, his normal guests wore the same orange red, so that was different."

"So, a transaction of a different type?"

"Again, yuck. But, yes. What if it was some sort of trade or blackmail happening? Could be that Jeremy had the stink on someone and was being paid off."

"If you're thinking she's the killer, then why murder him later?"

I shrugged. "Maybe he told the killer he'd be back for more money or something. And yes, I know, it's a reach and we have no evidence. I did text Lizzie to see if she by any chance remembered the color of the lipstick. She said it was pink, which means he was cheating."

"Well, we know that much from what Wallace and Aubrey said. Women can wear different kinds of lipsticks, right?"

"That's a good point. Though, most of us are partial to specific shades. I often wear a gloss or a lighter pink. With my hair, I look weird in other colors. But I thought it might give us some clue to add to what we already have. Dark-haired woman, and red lipstick. Not everyone can carry that color off."

"Can you think of anyone in Shamrock Cove? It occurred to me that we've been focused on residents, but we may need to widen our search. Since they were meeting at the hotel, they could have been coming from different towns."

"Ugh. It's always one step forward and three steps back."

"Right, but we also confirmed the affair, or affairs. And that he had a type."

"If that were the reason for his murder, you would think it might be Clara. But I just can't see her doing something like this. Even though she probably knew, given the lipstick on the collars, I can't see her murdering him. She's so tiny. Maybe one of the husbands or boyfriends?"

"Clara has an alibi for both murders. She was home with her kids. My team has gone over her and the family's alibis several times. Why would she kill her gran? It's obvious she loved her. By all accounts, she's a loving and caring woman. I do not think she would do anything to hurt her children, if nothing else."

"While it's usually a spouse, I agree with you. It makes me angry at Jeremy on her behalf though. He spent all of their money gambling and had the nerve to cheat. I mean..."

"I understand. Maybe, because of the finances she felt she couldn't make that break. That, and she is one who might stay because of the children," he said. "More often than not I run across victims who had to stay with a spouse for financial reasons."

"I fear you're right about that. Can we agree he wasn't a very good person?"

He laughed. "It's not my job to judge. I'm to gather evidence and a conviction. In this respect, he and his grand-mother-in-law are the victims. If we could figure out how the two murders are connected, other than the drug used, we could possibly find our killer."

"Maybe, and I'm just throwing it out there, it is about black-mail. What if Eva and Jeremy were in on it together? I understand that I didn't know her well, but I wouldn't put it past Eva to call someone out. Even if she wasn't in on the blackmail, Jeremy might have overheard something and decided to take advantage."

Kieran sighed loudly.

"You don't have to say it," I groaned. "We have no evidence to support any of that. Everyone says Eva was a gossip and was known for saying things for shock value, though. I mean, I've heard that from everyone. While I didn't know Jeremy either, he seems the type to take advantage if he could be prosperous."

"But who would have come into contact with both of them?"

"The woman with dark hair and red lipstick. She's about

five six, Aubrey remembered that as well. And the woman wore a floral scarf."

A face came into my mind. "No, it couldn't be."

"Who?"

Whoops. I hadn't realized I'd said that out loud.

I had someone in mind, but proving it was a whole other story. It was the lipstick color that stood out in my mind.

"Tell me," he asked.

I shook my head. "I was just thinking about the lipstick. There are a few women in town who wear something similar." One was Matt's mom, and the other was someone my sister swore it couldn't be. "I don't want to sound foolish. Give me some time."

By the time we arrived in Shamrock Cove, Kieran was annoyed with me because I wouldn't share the suspect. I had a few other things to check out first. He would need proof, and I was determined to find it.

That said, I couldn't imagine any of them committing either murder.

He pulled up in front of the bookstore. "Promise me you won't do anything dangerous."

"I won't. I promise."

"Please, tell me who you have in mind?" he said.

I grunted. "I want to, but it's so preposterous you'd laugh me out of the car. It's just that the physical description fits. I have no idea how they might be involved in all of this. It's a crazy reach and I honestly don't want you thinking I'm nuts."

"I would never do that."

I gave him the eye again. This time he was looking at me.

He sighed. "Fine. But make sure someone is with you when you're snooping this time."

"That's better." I patted his hand and then jumped out of the car before he could say anything else.

In the bookstore, Caro was checking out customers. Mr. Poe came around the counter to say hello. After I gave him some love, he led me to the back of the store. Lizzie was using a box cutter to open some boxes in the office.

"Hey, how did it go today?"

"Interesting."

"Oh, I know that tone. You have a killer in mind." She shivered. "Please tell me I don't know them."

"Wellll."

Her eyes went wide. "Who?"

"Stay with me on this, okay? You won't believe me but give me a chance to lay out all the facts."

She glanced at her watch. "Not here, let's go home for lunch. I don't want prying ears to hear you. Especially if you're going to name someone here in town. I have some vegetable soup and fresh bread from Paisley's waiting for us."

"Sounds good to me."

She let Caro know we were leaving and promised to bring her some lunch back.

Outside it was overcast and quite chilly.

"I hope the cold goes away in time for the fête. People will be freezing," she said.

"I think they're used to the chill here."

It wasn't long before we were in the house. Mr. Poe went straight to the back door for his afternoon romp.

I set the table, while Lizzie heated up the food on the AGA.

I made her a tea, and myself a cortado. I had a long day ahead.

When everything was ready, and Mr. Poe was back inside, we sat down.

"This soup is amazing."

"Thank you. It's all veg from the garden. I'm quite proud of myself. I did a bit of canning while you were gone. We'll have good veg all winter."

"You should be proud. This is delicious. I think it should go on the once-a-week roster."

She smiled. "That is saying something."

"Also, easy for me to heat up for lunch. When you aren't here, I can drink it out of a cup."

"And you will."

"Yep." I grinned.

"So, tell me this crazy idea you have."

"I don't have the 'why' yet. Though, I feel like it's right there on the tip of my tongue. Like my brain has seen the piece of the puzzle, but it's not quite in the right place."

"Okay, now I'm dying to know. Who is it?"

"Well, one of the women is Marianne. The other is Matt's mom, though I'm thinking Marianne. She was for sure on the scene at the bookstore."

Lizzie's eyes went wide, and she coughed into her napkin. "You and I both know it isn't Matt's mom. She wouldn't hurt anyone. And Marianne Gilbreth, church secretary and head of the fête? Are you—"

"I know. I know." I waved my hands. "She has dark hair and is fond of wine-red lipstick and a floral scarf."

"But the color on the collars of his shirts was more orange red." My sister appeared confused. I didn't blame her.

"Exactly. That's the physical description we received today. It made me wonder if it could be her."

"But why? If you gave me a list of suspects, she'd be at the bottom. I mean, I can't see her doing anything that might break a nail. She's very good at getting the rest of us to do her bidding without fuss."

"Exactly. She's good at manipulating people. What if—"

"No." My sister shook her head. "I always try to be

supportive of you and the theories you come up with, but this is too much."

"She was there the night of the book signing."

"Yes, but in one way or another, you've talked to almost everyone who was there. No one saw anything. I guarantee someone would have noticed if they'd seen Marianne giving Eva a shot of insulin. She's sophisticated and super classy. I just can't see her doing it. That, and how would she even know Jeremy?"

"What if she had an affair with him and Eva found out. Maybe, Eva threatened to tell everyone about Little Miss Perfect. And Jeremy might have been trying to blackmail her."

She snorted this time.

I sighed. I had to agree. Saying it out loud made it sound even more of a stretch.

"I wear red lipstick sometimes and I have dark hair. Are you going to make me a suspect?"

"Of course not. But remember when we were at the vigil?"

"How can I forget? You nearly gave me a heart attack when you hid upstairs."

"But as you gave Clara her sweater, she was seated by Marianne. Then Marianne said something to her, and Clara gave her a go-to-heck look."

"She did?"

I nodded. "You were behind them, but it was fast. Then Clara turned away from her to speak to one of her kids."

"I do remember Clara getting up right after that. She said she needed to freshen up."

"Right. Because she was upset. We need to know what Marianne said to her."

"We can't just ask. Did you tell Kieran all of this?"

"Nope. I understand how insane it sounds. But something in my gut tells me I'm right. I just don't have the why. Marianne is smart, and our killer is exactly that. Using insulin is actually kind of brilliant. If given more time before the bodies were found, it may have dissipated completely. It's possible that she didn't think anyone would find Eva's body until the next day. If it hadn't been for Mr. Poe being so anxious, we may not have.

"Same with the beach huts. He was stuck under there pretty well. If Mr. Poe had not found him, I'm not sure we would have seen the body."

She shivered.

"Also, she's slim but strong. The woman at the hotel said the dark-haired woman was about five six. Marianne has nice arms. I bet she works out."

"Pilates," Lizzie said. "She's always going on about it."

"Exactly. I'm not saying it's her. I'm just saying the opportunity is there. I saw the woman in the video. Her face was hidden, but the build, that's the same."

"But why? I mean, you're always going on about motive. Why would she do such awful things? She isn't the type to have a fling with someone like Jeremy. This sounds terrible, but she is a woman with standards. She still speaks about her dead husband like it just happened yesterday. I can't see her—"

I blew out a breath. "That's what I have to figure out. The why. I'm going to need everyone's help."

"What do you have planned?"

"About the wake tomorrow night..."

TWENTY-FIVE

The next night we headed to the pub. My sister was quite obviously nervous beside me. We'd had to leave Mr. Poe at home, and I thought, perhaps, that was why she rung her hands.

"He'll be okay for a few hours," I said gently.

She glanced up at me. "Who?"

"Mr. Poe. I know you both have separation anxiety, but there are times when it's best for him to stay home."

"What are you talking about?" She appeared genuinely perplexed.

"You seem nervous. You keep wringing your hands."

"Oh. It's not that."

"Tell me. Maybe I can help."

"I don't think so," she said, and it was more than obvious she was upset.

"Hey, you can tell me anything."

Outside the pub, she stopped. "I don't like your plan to disrupt the wake. These people are mourning loved ones. It all feels so disrespectful. I don't want to be a part of it."

I sighed. "Okay. I won't do it tonight."

"Really? Do you promise?"

"Absolutely. Lizzie, I would never do anything to upset you. I don't even know if she's going to be there. The more I think about it, you're right. This is hardly the time or place."

That said, I did plan to ask my suspects a few questions. If the opportunity presented itself.

We'd dressed in black in nearly identical outfits of slacks, sweaters and a white blouse underneath. Luckily, even though we were twins, we looked nothing alike. Her dark hair was piled on top of her head in a messy bun. My strawberry-blonde locks were down for once. I'd let Lizzie curl my hair for me.

If it weren't for her, I would never know anything about makeup or hair. She even coordinated my outfits for the book tour. It wasn't difficult, since most of my clothes were black.

Inside, Matt waved us toward the back. As expected, the front of the pub was fairly empty. He was carrying a tray of empty glasses.

"Is your mom busy?"

He frowned. "She is in the kitchen and we're a bit behind. What's up?"

"I wanted to ask her something about the case, but it can wait."

"I'll let her know."

"Thanks."

"You promised," Lizzie said beside me.

"Right. Sorry. I thought you meant about Marianne."

She rolled her eyes.

At the door to the big room at the back of the pub Lolly sat at a table with flowers and a guest book. There were several photos of Eva and Jeremy with the family spread about. "So happy you two could make it," she said. "It's kind of you to be here."

"Of course," Lizzie said. She signed us both in and we gave Lolly a brief wave. I'd only mentioned my plan to Rob and Brenna. Well, and Lizzie. But I'd made a promise to my sister.

It was crowded inside. My idea of torture. I'd never been a fan of rooms full of people. I could handle the book signings because there was usually a table between me and the readers. But this place was jam-packed.

As usual, we found Rob and Scott in one of the corners. Like me, Scott wasn't a fan of crowds.

"I thought you were out of town," I said to him when we walked up.

He grinned and we hugged. "I came back for the wakes and funerals. I set up the accounting system for Mrs. Walsh's farm and the store," he said. "They've been clients since we moved here."

"I didn't know," I said.

"She hadn't been feeling well for years, but Rob tells me it was murder for both of them?" He whispered the last bit.

"We aren't supposed to say anything." I gave Rob the eye.

He shrugged. "Technically, he's a part of the gang. Also, he's my husband."

"True," I said and smiled.

"Mercy promised me no talk of that tonight," Lizzie said.

The men glanced at one another and then me.

"Out of respect to the family," I said.

"When has that ever stopped you?" Rob asked.

I cleared my throat. "It's so crowded. We should go say something to the family."

"We'll come with you. They are in the far corner." Rob waved a hand that way. "Let's stick to the outside walls for yours and my luv's sake."

"Thank you," I said.

It took a few minutes, as we were stopped every few steps to say hello to people. Many of them were customers at the bookstore and my sister knew them all by name. I really did admire her ability to do that.

Clara and her children were seated at a round table near the stage at the front of the room. There were flowers and photos of Eva and Jeremy all around them and on the stage. The way things had been organized was beautiful and I said so.

Clara reached out to hug my sister, then me.

"Thank you both for coming," she said softly. It was obvious she'd been crying, and my heart broke for her. Any idea of looking for a killer among the family went out of my mind.

"Will you sit with us?" the oldest son, Kingston, asked. "I'd like to talk to you about my dad," he whispered.

"You have so many people who want to talk to you," I said. "But if you need a break, come and find me. I will probably be in a corner somewhere. I'm not great with crowds."

"Thanks," he said. "Maybe after the minister speaks?"

"I'll be here," I said. I wondered what he wanted to ask. I couldn't say anything about his father's death. Kieran, and my sister, would kill me.

Not long after we moved away from the table, we made it over to the row of food. Lizzie had fed us before we left the house, but there were petits fours from Paisley's bakery. I'd forgotten about her girls' day invite. I asked Lizzie about it.

"Oh, that was sweet of her. But we have the fête duties that afternoon, remember? It starts next weekend."

"I'd forgotten. I'll let her know."

"She sure can make pastries and bake," Lizzie said. "I could eat all of these little chocolate cakes."

"They are one of my favorites too," Paisley said from behind us. She carried a tray of more of the tiny delights.

"You are so talented," Lizzie said.

"The praise is well deserved," I said.

Paisley blushed. "You two are so good for my ego. Matt and his mom asked if I could help out, as there were more invited than they had been told."

"Matt said with the fête coming up, he needed all the help he could get."

"He's a good one," Lizzie said. "By the way, Mercy told me about the invite. We'd love to come, but we have meetings that afternoon for the fête."

Paisley's eyes went wide. "I think perhaps I may have a meeting that afternoon, as well. I completely forgot. I'm on the food committee with you." She hurriedly put the tray down and pulled her cell out of her pocket. "Thank goodness you said something. Marianne would have killed me. I missed the last food committee meeting here at the pub, and I thought she wanted my head. But we were slammed at the bakery that day. I couldn't get away."

Speaking of Marianne, I glanced around. I hadn't seen her in the crowd.

Interesting.

"Well, we hope for another invite," Lizzie said. "And glad we could help. Would you like me to help you put these on the tiered cake stand?"

"I've got it, thank you. Here." She put two more of the chocolate cakes on Lizzie's plate, for which she was thanked profusely by my sister.

We made our way to a table where Rob, Scott, Brenna and my sister's doctor friend sat.

"Rob mentioned you were here." Conor stood and pulled out the chair next to him for her.

My sister's cheeks were several shades of pink, and it had nothing to do with the blush she wore.

"Hi, Conor," she said softly. "I thought you'd be at work."

"I'm their family doctor," he said. "Of course I'd come. Though, I can't stay for long. I have a late shift at the hospital tonight."

Before we could say any more, a bell rang out. Then the minister moved behind the podium on the stage.

"Friends and family of Eva Walsh and Jeremy Lynch, please take your seats," he said.

He spoke about Eva first. It was funny that he brought up that she was never shy to say exactly what she meant. That he admired her honesty. After he finished about Eva, he said a few words about Jeremy, though not as much. It was clear he didn't know the man very well.

Then he invited others in the room to speak up.

Marianne bustled to the stage quickly. She held several sheets of paper in her hand. For someone who liked to keep meetings sharp and brief, she spoke for a long time. But I hardly listened as I focused on Clara. If looks could kill, Marianne would be dead.

Marianne who had dark hair and deep wine-red lipstick. The exact shade the woman at the hotel had mentioned.

I was right. I just had to prove it.

TWENTY-SIX

After Marianne, several people spoke about Eva. Many of them were from Lolly's book group. Then a few of Jeremy's friends stepped forward. They were a bit less eloquent, but they said kind things about him. While they spoke, Clara stared down at her hands.

When it was over, I wanted to speak with Marianne, but I'd made a promise to my sister. She made for the door, and I made excuses that I had to go to the ladies. Thankfully, my sister was enamored with her good doctor. I decided, technically, if I caught Marianne outside the pub, it wouldn't be during the wake. But a hand on my shoulder stopped me.

"Can I talk to you about something?" Kingston asked.

"I, um. Sure." He looked upset and I couldn't make an excuse. Marianne would have to wait. "Do you want to chat in here or out front?"

"Anywhere but here," he said. He shook his head.

I followed him out to the front of the pub, which had a few more people at the bar, but was still fairly empty. I motioned for him to sit down at my regular table. It was near the back with a view of the rest of the pub and no one was around.

"Is something wrong?" I asked.

He took a deep breath. "I know I wasn't particularly kind when you came out to the house."

"It's okay. You were all grieving."

"It's not that," he said. "The police won't say but I know Gran and my da were murdered. You help the police. Can you tell me anything?"

I made a face. "I do consult with the police sometimes, but if Kieran is keeping things close, he usually has a reason."

"But if he doesn't tell us, how can we help?"

"What do you mean?"

He stared down at his hands, which were on the table. "I want you to know my da wasn't a bad man."

"Okay."

"But he sometimes didn't make the best choices. I think Ma knows. Well, she definitely knows about the money. He lost it all. It's why we had to move in with Gran. I'm the only one who knows. Though I think Niamh has figured it out too."

I nodded.

"But Da... he sometimes..." His eyes filled with tears. "I don't know how he could do that to Ma. I was so mad when I found out. I tried to talk to him about it. He told me to mind me own. That I had no idea what I was talking about. But my friends have seen him in the pub here, and a few towns over.

"And I've been wondering..."

"What?" I asked softly.

"If, maybe, an angry husband might have killed him. Though I don't know why they would go after Gran. Unless she was some sort of warning to him."

"I—uh. Have you told Kieran your suspicions?"

"I tried. But Ma or Niamh are always around. I mean, I could be wrong about all of it. I find it all so suspicious that it happened so near together. Do you understand what I'm trying to say?"

"I do. You need to speak to Kieran though. Perhaps he can give you some answers and you can help him with his investigation. I'll go with you, if you'd like. I know it's a big deal to share something like this."

"Will you? Tomorrow morning?"

"Yes." I wrote my cell number on the napkin. "Text me when you're ready, and I'll meet you in front of the station."

"I should go back. Ma will be wondering where I am."

I nodded. "Did you ever see him with anyone?" I asked. It occurred to me that this young man was extremely protective of his family. I didn't see him as a suspect, but he might have seen something that didn't register at the time.

"No. I'm glad. I'm not sure what I'd have done if I caught him cheating on Ma. He was a good man, but what Gran would call weak. They were always at it. He and Gran, that is. Constantly fighting when we moved into her house. She never thought he was good enough for me ma."

He headed back inside. I was about to follow when I caught Marianne coming out of the back where the restrooms were. She headed quickly to the front door.

"Marianne." I waved.

Her shoulders stiffened, but she stopped.

As she turned, she pasted that smile that didn't quite go to her eyes on her face. "Oh, hello, Mercy. How are you?"

"Those were very kind words you shared about Eva," I said. "I know you two had your differences, but you speaking up for her was lovely."

She cleared her throat. "Of course I did. She was a dear friend. We may have fallen out, but that was years ago. No good holding on to all of that now. If you'll excuse me, it's been an emotional night."

"Yes, it has. I was curious about your relationship with Jeremy though."

"I've no idea what you're talking about. I only knew the

man through Eva and his wife Clara." Her eyes narrowed. "I don't think I like what you are suggesting, Mercy. That imagination of yours has run wild."

"I'm not suggesting anything. But Kieran has a photo of you at the hotel. The one that looks like a ski chalet."

Her mouth became a straight line.

"Impossible. I have no idea what you're talking about. I do not have to stand here listening to your wild imaginings. Go put your stories in a book and leave me alone." She turned on her heel and slammed out of the pub.

I was definitely on to something. Now, I had to prove it.

TWENTY-SEVEN

After making certain Kieran was at the station, I met Kingston in front of it. He hopped from foot to foot, nervously. When he saw me, he waved. "Thanks for coming," he said. "I appreciate it."

"Of course," I said. "Come on. I promise it will be painless."

Kieran hadn't been able to make the wake the night before as he'd been in Dublin following up on something, which he wouldn't share. But I'd texted him about this morning and he'd answered that he'd be in the office.

"He's waiting for you," Sheila said. "Can I get you a cuppa, Kingston? Anything for you, Mercy?"

"No, ma'am, thank you." He took his cap off. His nerves were palpable.

"I'm good," I said. If Sheila had made the coffee, it would burn a hole through my chest.

I led him down the hallway.

"I don't think I can do this," he whispered.

I put a hand on his shoulder. "It's okay, Kingston. Don't be scared."

Kieran stood when we knocked on the door. Then he motioned for us to sit down across from him.

"Mercy tells me you have something to share about your da?" He was calm, and smiled at the boy.

Kingston let loose then. His voice was full of emotion. "But you might not be on the right track if someone killed him. There has to be an angry husband or two. I didn't want to say anything in front of my mom or brother and sisters. They don't need to know the bad side. It would crush them."

"Do you by chance know any of the women he may have been seeing?"

The boy shook his head. "I only heard from my mates. I was so embarrassed and angry. I was away at uni when they texted me, they'd seen him a few towns over."

"Did they by chance send pictures?" I asked.

"Yes, but I deleted them. And all he was doing was sitting next to some woman at a pub."

"Do you remember what she looked like?"

He shrugged. "I only glanced at it but she looked nothing like Ma. I think she had dark hair. It was from behind, so I didn't see much."

"What made your friends think they were together?" Kieran asked.

"They walked out together, and they saw them kissing down the road."

He shook his head. "When I confronted Da, I told him everything. He said my friends were mistaken and I didn't know what I was talking about. It was just some woman who was in on his card game, and she tripped and fell into him. That's what they saw. I didn't believe a word of it.

"He was lying. But... I mean, he's my da. If he was cheating... I mean, a month later, he ends up dead. It just made me think, you know."

"I'll definitely look into it. Any chance you could put together a list of your friends who saw them in the pub?"

"They'll think I'm grassing on them."

"Kieran can be discreet," I said. "The more information, the better."

"What I don't understand is why they hurt Gran," the young man said. "She was funny, and like that lady said, and the minister, she always told people what she thought. I can't imagine someone wanting to hurt her. But that's the rumor. I think it's time you told our family what's really going on, or at least me. I'm the man of the house now. I can take it."

Kieran leaned back in his chair. "I've been waiting for the ME's test results to come in and the last of those should be in around noon. I was heading out to your place later to let your mom know. And your dad and gran will be released to the funeral home this afternoon."

"But it took so long because they were both murdered, right? Why else would you keep Gran?" Kingston was smart. "Her health wasn't great, but if it had been that we wouldn't have had to wait so long for her remains, and you wouldn't be searching the house."

Kieran nodded. "You're bright, Kingston. And you're right. I'd like to share everything with you and your mom at the same time. She's going to need you. Why don't you head home, and I'll let you know when I'm headed your way."

"Yes, sir. Thank you. And thank you." He turned to me. "I appreciate you keeping your word. You're right, he was nice." The young man stood and then walked out.

Kieran shook his head. "I feel sorry for him and his ma."

"Me too. Do you have any more answers about how they were killed?"

"Only that you were right. Jeremy was rolled under that beach hut. There are several abrasions that happened after his death."

"And they were definitely both poisoned with insulin?"

He nodded.

"Something happened last night, and I know you don't want to hear it, but can you give me the same respect you did Kingston?"

"I always do, Mercy."

"You sure?" I asked. My eyebrows went up.

He sighed.

"I told Marianne last night that you have a picture of her with Jeremy at the hotel. I thought she might explode. There is definitely something there."

"You did what?" His eyebrows disappeared into his hair. "I'm sure she was insulted. But, believe me, she has an airtight alibi. She was at the church with witnesses."

"Does she though? Jeremy was a lot healthier than Eva. She could have dosed him much earlier and the poison took longer to take effect. Also, her house is up on the cliffs above where the beach huts are."

"Mercy. Why would she risk killing two people? What's the motive? And you forget that Mr. McCormick owns the apothecary and held poker games on his boat."

I sighed and then I held up my hands. "Yes. I know it's her but I have no idea how she did it." But I was determined to figure it out.

TWENTY-EIGHT

After spending most of the morning going over every clue I'd discovered and writing down what Kieran had shared, I was about to give up. I decided to let it all go and focus on my current book. Sometimes I did that when writing, and things would come to me.

By six or so that evening, I'd written four chapters but was no closer to finding clues in the real-life case. Maybe I was wrong. But my gut wouldn't give up. It was Marianne, I just didn't know the why. Nor did I have any proof.

That, and Kieran said she had a strong alibi, but he'd never said what it was. I was about to text him when my phone beeped.

Mr. Poe needs a romp, Lizzie texted. *I've got young adult readers tonight.*

Be there soon, I texted back.

A short walk was what I needed to clear my mind. I headed out of the house and then looked to the left and right. I felt like someone might be watching, but none of the neighbors were outside.

I shook it off.

When I made it to the back door of the bookstore, I used my key. Caro was at the front desk. Lizzie was upstairs leading a discussion about whatever book the young adult group had chosen.

Mr. Poe wagged his tail so hard he made me laugh.

"Someone has been anxious tonight," Caro said.

"I've been writing, or I would have picked him up earlier. Thanks for watching him."

"It's always a pleasure. He's my favorite animal in the world."

Mr. Poe licked her shoe in thanks. We laughed.

I put his leash on his harness, and we headed out the back door. I made certain it was locked.

Again, I felt as though someone might be watching us, but Mr. Poe yanked on the leash. He was anxious to get home.

"If someone was there, you would notice," I said to him.

He pulled me toward the secret door.

I'd forgotten to pick up the mail by the door. I set it on the small table in the hall, but there was a large legal-sized envelope. I frowned. It was addressed to me and Lizzie.

Mr. Poe whined.

I unhooked his harness and then let him outside. While he was out there, I put food and water in his dishes. Then I opened the fridge to see what I might eat for dinner. When Lizzie was busy, I usually went down to the pub, but I didn't feel like socializing. My brain was too full of facts, and I needed time to sort through it all.

But I couldn't take my eyes off the big envelope. It was from a law firm. My stomach churned with worry. If it had been super official, we probably would have had to sign for it.

I didn't want to worry Lizzie, so I opened it. The letter stated they were trying to contact us about our father's estate. I was confused. We'd thought him dead long ago—or maybe, he really had been in hiding for some reason.

I tried the number of the lawyer but received a voicemail that she was on vacation for a month.

Ugh. That figured. She didn't even leave a forwarding number. People in Ireland took their vacations seriously and were usually gone for a month or more.

"Just when I thought we might get some answers. And why now?" The silence had no answers.

I looked at my watch. My sister would be home at seven. I put the letter in my room. Until I checked it out, I wouldn't worry her about it.

Besides, I had something else on my mind. Maybe I could show her why I'd been thinking about Marianne as the killer.

I fixed us both a sandwich and heated up some of the left-over veg soup from the other day. After setting places for us, I spread out the clues again on the table.

By the time I had everything set up, I realized Mr. Poe hadn't made a sound. It had been a good half hour.

I opened the door and was abruptly shoved back inside. I stumbled on the mat and hit my butt hard on the wood floor.

"What?"

In one hand, Marianne held Mr. Poe. In the other was a syringe.

I shook my head. "Don't hurt him. I'll do whatever you want, Marianne."

"Yes, you will," she said. "How dare you." She spit the words out.

"I don't understand," I said. I tried to stand up, but she moved the syringe closer to Mr. Poe.

"Stay there. Don't play dumb. You know why I'm here."

"I think I do. But I don't know why."

She glanced past me at the table. "Liar."

My stomach was in my throat. There was no way I'd let her hurt Mr. Poe, but I had to keep her talking. While she glanced at the table, I tried to dial 1 1 2 on the cell phone in my cardigan pocket.

"Please, there is no reason to hurt us," I said loudly, praying I'd hit the right numbers. I had to get Mr. Poe away from her and the needle. Better me than him. He was too small to hold up to all that insulin. If that was what was in the syringe.

I tried to stand up again.

"Move, and I'll fill him full of poison. He's small. He won't last."

Anger boiled inside of me. Who picked on a poor animal?

Awful people.

As her mask fell and the truth spilled out on her face, I understood she was more than desperate. And desperate people never thought clearly.

"We can work this out. I promise. You just need to tell me why."

"Stop playing dumb. You told me last night that you'd seen my picture with Jeremy."

"Yes, but I don't know *why* you were there."

"Don't you?" She sneered.

"Were you having an affair?"

She scoffed. "Never. It was a fling. One time and he and that greedy grandmother-in-law thought they could blackmail me. Can you believe that? Me? One drunken night—the only one since my husband died—and they expected me to pay for something I couldn't even remember very well."

"Are you saying he drugged you?"

She waved the hand with the needle. Mr. Poe squirmed, but she only held him tighter. Poor dog was probably very confused. "Nothing that sordid. I was at a pub a few towns over drowning my sorrows one Friday. I'd booked a hotel room out of town so I could let loose for one night and no one would be the wiser.

"Then *he* came along."

"Jeremy?"

She smirked again. "Your sister said you were bright. Keep up."

Ouch.

"He talked so sweetly. Said he'd always fancied me. He even used that word. I wasn't thinking clearly. I'd had three too many Chardonnays trying to bluster the courage to ask a bloke to dance. But Jeremy made it easy."

"And then he blackmailed you?"

"I've no idea how Eva found out. It was like when she accused me of killing my husband, which was true."

"You killed him?"

"Of course I did, but you aren't listening to me," she said. "That old woman kept whispering that she knew what I did. But she'd never come out and say it. I couldn't have imagined Jeremy told her. She hated him, but there was only one way to make sure. And I couldn't be sure if it was Jeremy or my husband she was talking about. I had to get rid of her before someone actually listened to her ramblings. Then she made that comment at your bookstore about you and Kieran being single and gave me a pointed stare. I knew it."

"You killed her that night at the bookstore."

"I didn't realize it would kill her so fast. I expected her to go home and die in her sleep. No one would have been the wiser. The insulin would have worn off and everyone would have assumed it was her time. Just my luck. I hadn't meant to kill her right away.

"It was only a matter of time before she told the world. I didn't think anyone in this town would think it was murder. I mean, she was old and ailing."

I wasn't about to mention I was the one who suggested they test quickly for toxins.

"I don't think she knew about you and Jeremy," I said.

She frowned. "What? But she threatened me."

"Did she? Or did she pick on you like she did most people?

Perhaps she suspected about your husband and wanted to give you a hard time. But you felt guilty and took it the wrong way. From what I understand, she liked to stir up trouble. She resented your perfection. A lot of people do. You were never really friends, were you? She never let up, she just didn't do it as much in public. Small private comments that wore you down."

"But..." She appeared confused. "How can you know that?"

"She never asked you for money, right?"

She shook her head.

"Jeremy's the one who actually blackmailed you. Did he say he had photos or something?"

"Yes." She sounded uncertain. "He showed me on his phone. I thought that meant he knew I killed her. That's what he insinuated when we met at the hotel."

"I think you assumed too much. Did he actually say he thought you killed his grandmother-in-law?"

She seemed to think about it. Then she shook her head.

"He was going to blackmail you for sleeping with him. But you could have just said no. You're a single woman. He was a married man. It would have been much worse for him if Clara knew."

"I never meant to hurt Clara. She was so kind when my husband died. But her family, they were awful people. They were going to ruin everything for me. My reputation is all I have left. People think I'm a pillar of the community."

"They do, but you fell for his blackmail plans. You planned all this so carefully," I said.

"How would you know?"

"You wrote about it in your manuscript. I read it. The writing was excellent, by the way. At the very least, you'll win an honorable mention."

"Really?" She seemed surprised by the news. "I wrote it before any of this happened. I mean, I'd slept with Jeremy. But then he made threats. I planned it, but I wasn't going to really do it. But Eva said that, and I had to take action. I didn't think I'd have the courage to kill him, let alone her. It was easier than I expected. I pretended to hug them. She didn't even feel it. He thought I'd pinched him."

She was past the point of listening. I had to get my dog away from her.

He whined.

"Quiet," she said.

Then he growled.

She raised her hand as if she were going to stab him, and then all at once she pitched forward. I caught Mr. Poe as her arms windmilled and she tried to find purchase, she slammed into the wall and then flat on her face with an 'oomph'.

Standing behind her was my sister. "You threatened my dog," Lizzie said angrily. She was about to kick her, when Kieran slid into the room behind me. He quickly pulled me to my feet.

"It's okay, Lizzie. We have her," Kieran said.

Then Sheila came in. She put her knee on Marianne's back and read her her rights. "You are under arrest..." Sheila yanked her up none too gently and shoved her toward the front door.

I squeezed Mr. Poe tight, and he licked my face. "You were a very brave boy."

"You both were," my sister said. Then she wrapped her arms around me.

"How did you know?"

"When I opened the front door I could hear you. I called Kieran, and then I went through Rob's house to the backyard."

"I have part of her confession on my phone," Rob said as he stepped from behind Lizzie.

I laughed. "I wish I knew you guys were there. I was scared to death for Mr. Poe."

"Oh, I wouldn't have let her hurt either of you. I'm just mad I didn't believe you," Lizzie said.

"How did you knock her down?"

"After the last time we were attacked, you showed me all those self-defense moves. I elbowed her in the kidney and kicked her behind the knees. My arm hurts, but it was worth it." She took Mr. Poe from me. "And Mercy is right. You were a brave boy."

I laughed and couldn't stop.

Kieran had his hand on my shoulder. He turned me to face him. "Are you really, okay? Did she stab you with the syringe?"

I pointed to the floor. "It rolled under the table. She killed her husband."

He pulled me to him and squeezed hard. "I heard. I thought she'd stuck you with it."

My arms were trapped in his hug.

"I'm fine," I whispered.

"Still, you're going to the hospital," he said. He didn't let me go. "Scared the life from me."

"The only thing that hurts is my bum, and my pride. She got the better of me with that surprise. I didn't see her coming."

"Why am I shaking?" Lizzie asked.

"Adrenaline and shock," Rob said. "You sit down. I'll make you a cuppa."

The next several minutes were all of us talking over one another as we went over the details. Then Lolly and Brenna arrived with cookies and cakes. Not long after, Dr. Conor knocked on the door. He insisted on checking us both out.

Hours later, Lizzie and I tiredly ushered them out the door. Kieran was the last to leave, and my sister left us at the front door.

"You scared me," he said.

"I didn't go after trouble this time, I swear." Okay, maybe

confronting her at the pub hadn't been the smartest idea. "It showed up on my doorstep."

"You're like a magnet in that way."

I shrugged. "Any chance I can listen in when you question her?"

"You heard her confession. And it won't be until later tomorrow. I want her to sit and think about what she's done."

"Oh, that reminds me. Did you pick up the syringe?"

He nodded and then patted his pocket. "I'm taking it to evidence now."

I blew out a breath. "Thank you, Kieran, for showing up."

He smiled. "I was already on the way when your sister called. It was smart of you to dial emergency services. Sheila texted me as well. We've taped the whole conversation; she won't be able to go back on her word."

I laughed.

"What?"

"I had no idea if I dialed the right number."

"You did. Now, brace yourself."

"Wh—" Then his lips were on mine. My breath caught in my chest, and my eyes shut, and a delightful shiver slid down my spine.

Oh. My.

He let go of me. "I'll see you tomorrow." Then he walked away.

I put my hand on my lips. Kieran had kissed me.

And I liked it—a lot.

TWENTY-NINE
ONE WEEK LATER

The Autumn Festival was in full swing, and my sister had taken over for Marianne. In her kind, but full-of-strength way, she coordinated everything seamlessly. Everyone stopped us on the way to the party saying that it was the best fête yet. My sister beamed.

Ten minutes later, she was in the arms of Doctor Conor, who only had eyes for her. As they danced, her smile grew. Her cheeks were pink, and I hadn't seen her this happy in months.

"You're thinking about something," Kieran whispered beside me.

"No. Just watching happiness blossom."

He glanced out at the floor. "Ah. How about we join them?"

"In public? People will talk," I said.

He shrugged. "Do we really care?"

I laughed. "I don't."

"Come on." He pulled me out onto the floor. Thankfully, it was a slow number.

Lolly and Harold McCormick danced past us. "About time," she said.

Kieran and I laughed.

"I think she approves," he said.

"I'm quite the catch," I said.

"You are. Smart. Beautiful and a magnet for trouble." He gently slid his fingers across my cheek.

"No one is perfect."

"Least of all me, I should have listened to you."

"Not that again. You were right. I didn't have proof or a motive. At least, not before she showed up at my door. But please, don't let her ruin our evening. I'm actually having fun."

He grinned. He really did have a wonderful smile.

Life was good in Shamrock Cove and I had a feeling it would only get better.

A LETTER FROM LUCY CONNELLY

Lovely reader,

Thank you for choosing to read *A Body at the Irish Book Club*. If you enjoyed it, and would like to keep up with what is next, please sign up at the following link. Your email will never be shared, and you can unsubscribe at any time.

www.bookouture.com/lucy-connelly

I love that there is always something to celebrate in the fictional town Shamrock Cove, and that Mercy and her sister, Lizzie, are in the center of it all. I love the people who populate this small town. Do you have a favorite? I will never tell, but I have more than one.

I'd love to hear what you think. Please follow me on social media and write a review. It makes a big difference for readers looking for new authors to find those reviews. And please get in touch through my social media or website.

Love to you all!

Lucy Connelly

KEEP IN TOUCH WITH LUCY

www.lucyconnelly.com

 facebook.com/LucyConnellyBooks

 x.com/candacehavens

 instagram.com/candace_havens

ACKNOWLEDGMENTS

A big thanks to my editor Brittany Golob for her wonderful guidance with this book. Everyone at Bookouture, I adore you all. Thank you for making each experience better than the one before. You are an amazing team.

A shout out to my ever-patient agent, Jill Marsal, for telling me to try writing mysteries. You were right, it is my jam.

Readers, everything I write is for you. Thank you for the kind words and encouragement. Without you, none of this would be possible.

And to my friends Lizzie Bailey and David Faulkner, thank you both for always being there when I need you. I'm so lucky to have you in my life.

PUBLISHING TEAM

Turning a manuscript into a book requires the efforts of many people. The publishing team at Bookouture would like to acknowledge everyone who contributed to this publication.

Audio
Alba Proko

Commercial
Lauren Morrissette
Hannah Richmond
Imogen Allport

Cover design
Lisa Horton

Data and analysis
Mark Alder
Mohamed Bussuri

Editorial
Brittany Golob
Ria Clare

Copyeditor
Jane Eastgate

RAISING READERS
Books Build Bright Futures

Dear Reader,

We'd love your attention for one more page to tell you about the crisis in children's reading, and what we can all do.

Studies have shown that reading for fun is the **single biggest predictor of a child's future life chances** – more than family circumstance, parents' educational background or income. It improves academic results, mental health, wealth, communication skills, ambition and happiness.

The number of children reading for fun is in rapid decline. Young people have a lot of competition for their time, and a worryingly high number do not have a single book at home.

Hachette works extensively with schools, libraries and literacy charities, but here are some ways we can all raise more readers:

- Reading to children for just 10 minutes a day makes a difference
- Don't give up if children aren't regular readers – there will be books for them!

- Visit bookshops and libraries to get recommendations
- Encourage them to listen to audiobooks
- Support school libraries
- Give books as gifts

There's a lot more information about how to encourage children to read on our websites: **www.RaisingReaders.co.uk** and **www.JoinRaisingReaders.com**.

Thank you for reading.

Made in United States
Orlando, FL
11 May 2026